THE WITCHING OF
BEN WAGNER

The Witching of Ben Wagner

Mary Jane Auch

Houghton Mifflin Company
Boston 1987

Library of Congress Cataloging-in-Publication Data

Auch, Mary Jane.
   The witching of Ben Wagner.

   Summary: When twelve-year-old Ben moves with his
family to a town on the shore of Lake Ontario he finds
a friend who seems to be a witch and who helps him
meet the problems associated with his moving and with
his stormy relationships with his father and big sister.
   [1. Moving, Household — Fiction. 2. Family life —
Fiction. 3. Ontario, Lake
(N.Y. and Ont.) — Fiction] I. Title.
PZ7.A898Wi 1987   [Fic]   87-14999
ISBN 0-395-44522-1

Printed in the United States of America

S 10 9 8 7 6 5 4 3 2 1

For Natalie, my mentor and friend

THE WITCHING OF
BEN WAGNER

1

They say your whole life passes in front of you when you're dying. That's exactly what it felt like the day we moved out of Phillipsburg, as all the things I'd known for the whole twelve years of my life whisked by me and disappeared.

Dad caught my eye in the rearview mirror. "Ben? Did you move the last of that trash out to the road so it'll get picked up in the morning?"

"Yes, sir," I said.

"What about the house keys? Did you remember to take them next door to the Olafsens'?"

"Sure, Dad. They said they'd give them to the Realtor for you."

Dad stopped watching me and turned his attention back to the road. I could tell he was still mentally checking off the list of things that had to be done before we left, most of which involved me, in one way or another. I always seemed to get stuck with more of the work than either of my sisters.

My little sister, Liz, was pretty upset about moving. "Daddy, can we go back so I can check my room one more time?" she asked. "Maybe I forgot something."

"I'm sure there wasn't anything in your room, Liz," Mom said, putting her arm around Liz. "We checked it several times. Remember?"

"Well, I could have left something outside of my room. Maybe even outside of the house. If we could stay around a few more days I could look around real hard just to make sure."

Dad patted Liz on the head. "I know it isn't easy to move away from your home, pumpkin, but we don't have any choice. A man has to make a living and I can't do that here anymore. You're going to like Lakeview, though. My new barbershop has a little store in it, with candy and comic books. How does that sound?"

"Okay, I guess." Liz slumped back down in her seat.

We passed my best friend Herbie's big, sprawling dairy farm on the hill outside town. I knew every inch of that place. I had spent a lot of time there, helping Herbie with his chores, and generally messing around. I twisted around in my seat to see it for as long as I could. I had a weird feeling that as long as I could keep Phillipsburg in view, we wouldn't really be leaving. I imagined there was a big rubber band that ran from the town to the rear bumper of the car. While I could still see the town, the

2

rubber band kept stretching and stretching. Then we went up over a hill and, as we dropped down into the next valley, the rubber band snapped. I felt a part of me zinging right back to Phillipsburg.

I turned back around in my seat to watch the road up ahead. I felt completely powerless, as if I'd been taken hostage. All I knew about Lakeview was that it was a suburb of Rochester, right on the shore of Lake Ontario. It might as well have been on the moon, as far as I was concerned.

Liz was getting itchy already. "Are we almost there, Daddy?"

"Not by a long shot, Liz. You might as well settle down. We have several hours on the road still ahead of us."

We'd been riding about ten minutes and the car was starting to get hot, so I rolled down my window. Susan, my older sister, started clutching her head and yelling at me. "Ben, put that window back up! You're blowing my hair all to pieces."

"Aw, come on Susan, it's sweltering in here," I countered.

Susan bent forward with her head behind Mom's seat, still holding her precious hairdo, which hadn't looked all that great when she got into the car. It was one of those dippy things she'd copied from a magazine. "Mother, please make Ben roll up the window."

Dad spoke up first. "Ben's right, Susan. You can't take a trip in August with the windows rolled up. You'll just have to comb your hair when we get there."

I couldn't believe Dad stuck up for me. Usually Susan

3

got her own way about everything. Now she was being a big martyr, still all bent over with her head on her knees. I hoped she'd get stuck in that position.

Liz kept trying to tune in radio stations, but none of them came in very clearly because of the mountains. Dad finally got sick of listening to static and told her to knock it off. Then she got bored and turned around in her seat to stare at Susan and me. It didn't bother me, but Susan, who had decided to sit back up and let her hair blow, got all bent out of shape about it. "Mom, please make Liz stop looking at me like that."

"Like what? I'm just looking. Can't a person look?"

"Mother, please make her stop."

Mom tugged Liz's arm. "Quick, honey, turn around and see the horses up ahead. There's one the color you like. What do you call that color?"

Liz turned around. "Ooh, palomino. He's beautiful." Mom is smart. She knows she can get a lot farther with Liz if she changes the subject instead of scolding. I wish Dad would learn that. He always yells before he thinks about what he's going to say.

I slipped my arm out the window and rested my hand on the roof of the car. Last year my arm hadn't been long enough to do that. By just raising my hand off the roof, I could feel the pressure of the wind against it. I had to be careful, because Dad would yell if he saw my arm out the window in his rearview mirror. One of the few funny things I ever heard Dad say to us was, "Don't stick your elbow out too far. It may go home in another car."

I was still experimenting with lifting and dropping my

hand, letting it flap in the wind, when suddenly there was a strange sound, a sort of *thup-thup-thup*. For a few seconds, I thought something awful had happened to my hand, and I waited for the pain to hit, but there wasn't any. Then Dad let loose with a whole string of words that he'd told us never to use, and he pulled the car over to the edge of the road. He got out and used some words I'd never even heard before when he saw the front tire on the passenger side. It was completely flat.

"Ben, get out here and help me," Dad barked. He's never quite gotten over the years he spent as a Marine drill sergeant. I jumped out and started hauling stuff out of the trunk to get to the spare tire.

Dad bellowed again, "Ben, get that jack over here on the double. Let's get going or we'll be here all day." I took the jack up to him while the others climbed out of the car to get some air.

Dad was working real hard to loosen one of the lugs on the wheel. The only trouble was, I was pretty sure he was turning it in the wrong direction. I knew because Herbie and I used to practice changing the tires on an old car behind their barn.

"Dad, I think you're turning it the wrong way," I said, kind of quietly.

Dad looked up at me, his face red from the effort. "What?"

"The lug wrench. I think you're turning it the wrong way. You're making it tighter instead of looser." That was probably more than I'd ever said to my father at one

5

time. Dad wasn't impressed. His face turned an even darker shade of red.

"So now you're a mechanic, are you? If you're going to criticize instead of help, just get out of the way and let me work." With that, he put his foot on the lug wrench and jumped up, bringing his whole weight down on it. There was a loud squeak, and I figured that lug must have been almost welded to the wheel by then, so I got out of there before Dad could figure out that I'd been right. He always gets a whole lot madder when somebody proves him wrong.

I went around the car and leaned against the back bumper next to Mom. Looking back down the road, you could see waves of heat coming up off the pavement, making the trees and farm down the road look all squiggly. The smell of melting asphalt was sharp in my nose and I could feel the sweat trickling down the back of my neck.

"I'm getting out of Dad's way, Mom. Let me know when you're ready."

Mom smiled. "That's probably a good idea. Stay within calling distance, though."

A row of tall bushes and close-packed trees blocked the view along the side of the road, but I could see light coming through, so I knew there was open space beyond it. I walked along the road until I came to a break in the bushes. A narrow path plunged down suddenly to a stream, glinting here and there where streaks of sunlight cut through the roof of leaves.

It must have been twenty degrees cooler in the shade than it was out on the pavement. I bent down and scooped up some water to splash over my head, then pulled off my sneakers and socks and sat on a big, flat rock with my toes wiggling in the cool stream. It was good to be by myself for a change. Our family had enough trouble getting along when we could spread out through a whole house. I wasn't looking forward to spending the next few hours jammed into a car with them. I just sat there for a long time.

Pretty soon there was a thrashing sound behind me and Liz came skidding down the path. "I wondered where you were, Ben. Why didn't you take me with you?"

"Because I wanted to be alone and have a little peace, that's why." Liz looked hurt when I said that, so I added, "You can sit here with me, Liz, but just be quiet for a minute, okay?"

Liz brightened up. "Oh sure, Ben. How will I know?"

"What?"

"How will I know when the quiet minute is up?"

"I'll let you know."

"Okay."

Liz saw my feet in the water and started fussing with the laces of her sneakers. "Ben?"

"Yeah?"

"I can't get my shoelaces untied. Don't start the quiet minute yet."

"Put your feet over here. I'll untie them." Liz swung her feet up into my lap and I got the knots out for her. "All right," I said. "We're starting now. Just be quiet, and listen for all the sounds you can hear." This was the only way I knew to keep Liz from chattering constantly.

7

She nodded solemnly, folded her hands in her lap, and closed her eyes. The first sound we heard was Dad using those words again in the distance.

She opened one eye and looked up at me. "That sound doesn't count, does it?"

"No, ignore that one."

"I thought so." Both eyes closed again.

I let out a deep breath and started listening. The stream was a small one, and didn't make any noise at all in the glassy part where it slid by. A little farther downstream, several peaks of rock jutted up, slicing the water into a pattern that looked like fishbones. That was where the sound came from, almost like Mom pouring Dad's morning cup of coffee.

Once you got past the water sounds, there were all kinds of noises coming from the pasture beyond the stream. A couple of locusts talked back and forth to each other with their raspy voices. There was the buzz of some honeybees working a patch of clover in the pasture, and in the far distance a dog was barking, with a little echo at the end of each woof, like a question mark.

I could feel Liz ticking like a little alarm clock about to go off. I didn't realize she'd been holding her breath until she let it out with a puff. "Ben, is the minute over yet?"

"Yeah, it's over. What kinds of sounds did you hear?"

Liz wrinkled up her nose. "I can't remember. I don't think I heard anything at all."

I wasn't surprised. It probably took all of her concentration just to stay quiet. Even though Liz was a pain in the neck sometimes, I really did like her. She never tried to be anybody but herself, not like pain-in-the-neck Susan. Maybe she'd been just as cute as Liz at one time. That was a pretty scary thought.

Liz's voice brought me back to the stream. "Ben, look! There are spiders dancing on the water."

"They're not spiders, Liz. I'm not sure what their real name is, but Herbie and I always call them water bugs."

They did look like spiders, though, with long, jointed legs that formed a big "X" at the middle of their bodies. They moved around on top of the water, their feet making little circle-shaped dips in the surface. They moved suddenly by kicking their legs so fast you couldn't even see it happen. It always made me feel that my eyes were blinking, but I knew they weren't.

"That's so sad, Ben."

"What's sad?"

"If those bugs stop kicking they'll be carried along with the water. They have to work so hard just to stay in one place."

I watched the bugs fighting the lazy current of the stream and knew exactly how they must feel. It seemed as if I was always working real hard just to keep from going backward. The older I got, the more Dad expected from me, and I was never able to measure up. I'd just learn how to do one thing, and he'd already be bugging me to start working on something else.

It was the same thing in school. I wasn't dumb, exactly, but I didn't always get the hang of what we were supposed to be learning. Not like Susan. She always got straight A's in everything. Starting out in a new school would be a cinch for her. I'd been worried about moving up to seventh grade in Phillipsburg, even though I knew a lot of the teachers and had been in class with most of the kids all my life.

Now everything was changed. I didn't have any control over what was happening to me. I had the feeling that this next school year I'd be working as hard as I could just to keep from being swept downstream.

"Ben! Liz! Get back here or we'll leave you behind." It was Dad, bellowing in the distance.

Liz looked up at me. "Let's just stay here, Ben. Then we wouldn't have to move, and we could go back to Phillipsburg."

I put my arm around her shoulders and gave her a half hug. "Don't worry, Liz. We'll be okay in the new place. We'll just have to stick together."

"Is it really going to be all right? You promise?"

"I promise."

I just wished I could believe it.

2

Spending a whole day cooped up in a car with my family was as bad as I thought it would be. It was the longest trip I'd ever been on in my life. Dad was still mad about the tire and didn't say much for the next couple of hours. After a while we passed beyond the hills, and the land seemed to flatten out as we headed upstate. Then we pulled onto an expressway, and the miles dropped away fast. As we came around a curve and over a rise, we could see a city in the distance.

"There's Rochester, but we won't go through it," Dad said. "The expressway by-passes it."

My stomach started to feel funny as I watched the cluster of tall city buildings get closer. This could be where I would spend the rest of my life, or at least my school years. I could already tell I was going to miss the hills.

The expressway split into several branches and got very confusing, with lanes of traffic crossing each other. Dad muttered something under his breath as the car to our right suddenly darted in front of him. "They call this mess the 'can of worms.' What kind of an idiot designs two highways that cross each other with no traffic lights?"

The expressway had taken us around the center of the city and the tall buildings were behind us. Now we were going past a section where the houses were close together, but at least there were lots of trees. It didn't look like the cities you see on TV, with just sidewalks and fire hydrants.

By the time we turned off at the exit for Lakeview, it didn't look like a city anymore at all. It was more like a small town, with a couple of blocks of stores, and houses packed in pretty close together down the side streets. It wasn't too different from the center of Phillipsburg, except here you couldn't look up and see the hills in the distance with barns and silos and herds of grazing cows.

Dad pointed to a dark brick building with a large playground. "There's your new school, Liz." A bunch of kids about Liz's age were playing baseball.

Liz scrunched down in the seat. "It's ugly."

Susan reached over the seat to pat Liz on the head. "You can't tell anything by the way it looks, Liz. There seem to be a lot of children your age. Maybe your new best friend is on that playground right now."

"No best friend of mine is going to play baseball. It's a dumb game."

Seeing that she wasn't getting anywhere with Liz, Susan

changed the subject. "Where will Ben and I be going to school, Dad?"

"The high school has grades seven through twelve, so you'll both be going there. The school is a pretty good distance from here, back toward the city, so you'll have to take the bus. I'll show you later. Right now, I want you to see the shop." Dad had pulled back onto the main street.

"I see it, Daddy," Liz shouted. "It has a real barber pole, like a giant peppermint stick."

Sure enough, there was a small shop with a sign that said ANGELO'S BARBER SHOP. On the front of the building, right next to the door, was a rotating red-and-white barber pole with a gleaming silver knob on top. Dad had always wanted a pole like that, but said they were too expensive. I wondered if he'd picked this shop because it came with a pole.

Dad skipped the space in front of the shop, and parked farther down the street. "Have to leave the good spots for the paying customers. Some people won't bother to stop for a haircut if they have to park too far away."

Dad seemed excited as he led us into the shop. I could tell he felt good about our future here. A short fat man was doing a haircut as we walked in. The man turned around when he heard the bell over the door jingle. He put down his scissors and came over to shake Dad's hand.

"George, I'm glad to see you again. This must be your beautiful family." His eyes swept over all of us as as he talked.

"I was anxious to get back to Lakeview, Angie. I'd like

you to meet my wife, Helen, my daughters, Susan and Liz, and my son, Ben. This is Angelo Romano, the man who's selling the barbershop to me."

Mr. Romano went down the line shaking hands, and when he got to me, he said, "Is this the next barber in the family?"

I'd never even thought about being a barber, or anything else for that matter. Luckily I didn't have to come up with an answer because Dad spoke up. "He just might be, Angie. Maybe he'll be a snip off the old block." They both laughed.

I tried to picture myself as a barber — a barber who couldn't talk. Dad always said that being able to cut hair was only half of his job. The rest was being able to carry on a good conversation with his customers.

I wandered off to look around. The barbershop part took up only about half of the room. The right-hand wall had a big mirror and a counter with two barber chairs in front of it. There was a man waiting for a haircut in the second chair, and two more men waiting in the seats up by the front window.

The rest was like a little store. There was a big magazine rack across the back that even had some of those magazines like the ones Herbie's older brother had hidden in the hayloft. I saw Mom's eyebrows go up when she spotted them. There were also sports and car magazines and a rotating rack filled with comic books. At the front of the store, across from the barber chairs, was a display case filled with candy bars, cough drops, gum, cigars, chewing tobacco, and jackknives. There was a cash

14

register on one end of the case, a pile of newspapers on the other, and two big glass jars with penny candy in the middle. The wall behind it had little cubbyholes filled with different brands of cigarettes.

Mr. Romano saw me eyeing the candy case. "Help yourself to a candy bar, Ben. You too, girls. You must be hungry after your long trip."

Liz's eyes grew wide and she looked up at Mom to see if it was okay. Mom nodded.

We slid open the glass door in back of the candy case. Liz and I each took a Milky Way and Susan took a bag of Reese's Pieces. Susan always chose something that she could make last for a long time, so she could gloat over Liz and me when ours was all gone. She usually ate about one Reese's Piece every fifteen minutes. I could never do that, no matter how hard I tried. I could start out with one at a time, but then I'd end up shoving handfuls of them into my mouth, and they'd disappear in a few gulps.

I glanced up and saw Mom looking at us with that raised-eyebrow expression that meant, "Say thank you." I elbowed Liz and we both mumbled our thanks, but Susan had to go into a whole speech about how wonderful the shop was, and how nice Mr. Romano was, and how glad she was to be moving to Lakeview. All the adults in the room were beaming at her. Susan was such a rotten phony, but grown-ups could never see through that kind of garbage.

Dad put his arm around Susan. "You keep your eye on this one, Angie. I wouldn't be surprised if she became our first woman president. She's got more brains than all

15

the rest of us put together. Never brought home a report card yet that didn't have all A's on it."

He gave Susan's shoulder a squeeze and she flashed that drippy smile of hers. "Oh, Daddy, you're embarrassing me."

I suddenly realized that my Milky Way was gone already. Susan gave me a sly little smirk as she placed a Reese's Piece on the tip of her tongue and closed her mouth so slowly you could just tell she was going let it melt all the way down to nothing without ever biting into it.

All of a sudden I had to get out of there. "I'm going to go outside and look around, Dad. Okay?"

"All right, Ben. I want to stay here and talk to Angie, and I have to call the real estate agent so he can bring over the keys to the house. Be back here in about twenty minutes."

Mr. Romano led me up to the front window. "You should go see Lake Ontario, Ben. It's only a short walk from here. Just keep going to where the road curves to the right. There's a path that goes up over the embankment and you can get to the lake from there. The ladies might be interested in some of the shops back along the road in the other direction."

Susan got all excited. "Oh, could we, Mother? We passed the cutest little boutique just down the road."

"I guess so," Mom agreed. "But let's remember, our main purpose here is to get settled in, not buy clothes."

Liz took my hand and looked up at me. "Please take

me with you, Ben," she whispered. "I want to see the lake, not some old shop."

I'd had my heart set on a little exploring by myself, but Liz looked so miserable, I couldn't say no. "Liz is going with me, Mom. Okay?"

Susan answered for her. "That's much better. I can't stand dragging a baby along when we shop." Then she cut herself off fast, realizing she had shown her true colors to all the people she had just impressed. "I mean, it wouldn't be fair to Liz. She's so tired from the trip."

Liz and I left the shop and started down the road.

"Mr. Romano made me mad," Liz said.

"Why? He's a nice guy. He even gave you a candy bar."

"Because he only asked if you were going to be a barber. He never even asked if I wanted to be one."

"Do you?" I asked.

"No. I want to be a race car driver and a ballerina, but I could be a barber if I wanted to. Mom even lets me use her scissors with the pointy ends now. I'm very careful."

"You'd make a great barber, Liz." Why not? Liz could talk anybody's ear off.

Liz and I kept walking toward the lake, even though we couldn't see any sign of it from where we were. It was a funny little town, a drugstore and a small grocery after the barbershop, then an empty lot and an autobody shop. There was a whole string of small shops on the other side of the street. Then, after the traffic light,

17

there was the fanciest miniature golf course I'd ever seen, with all kinds of little castles and buildings made out of stones.

Liz spotted it the same time I did. "Oh, Ben, look at that beautiful little town. It's just the right size to play dolls in. Can we go look?"

"We don't have time right now. Besides, you have to pay to get in. And it's for playing golf, not dolls."

Liz's face dropped.

"Look, I'll take you in there one of these days, even give you a miniature golf lesson, okay?"

"I guess so. But where's the lake? I bet there isn't one. Mr. Romano probably makes up stories, too."

There was a steep bank on the other side of the road where it curved, with a path worn in it, just like Mr. Romano said. I took Liz's hand crossing the road and we scrambled to the top.

Suddenly, there it was. As far as we could see, in all directions, there was nothing but water, miles and miles of it. I'd never been able to see that far into the distance in my whole life. Liz was speechless for a couple of minutes. When she finally spoke, it was barely a whisper. "Ben, the lake doesn't have any other edges but this one. What happened to the other side?"

"It's there, Liz. It's just too far away to see. That's Canada over there somewhere."

We skidded down the slope, down to the edge of the water. There wasn't any sand, just millions of different colored round stones. Every now and then the lake slid a small wave up on the rocks.

Liz moved closer to me and took my hand. "Ben, I'm scared. It's too big."

I gave her hand a squeeze. "Don't be silly, Liz. The lake can't hurt you. It's just a big puddle of water."

Suddenly, as if challenging me, the lake slipped a wave over our feet, soaking us up to the ankles.

3

Getting moved into the new house wasn't easy because it was a lot smaller than the old one. It was like most of the other houses in Lakeview, square and ugly, more of a summer cottage than a real house. There was no yard to speak of in the front, and the back yard was almost completely filled by our big old redwood picnic table. I was used to a back yard the size of a soccer field.

Inside the house, on the first floor, there was a living room in front and a kitchen in back. The second floor held three small bedrooms and the only bathroom. My room was in the attic, and the only part of it I could stand up in was the middle, because the ceiling slanted down on both sides. There was one window, but all I could see from it were the tops of trees and the roofs of other houses.

I missed the view from my old room in Phillipsburg, where I could see the top of Frew Run Hill and the mountains beyond it.

I think the only one who really liked the new house was Liz, who had her own room for the first time in her life. She had her dolls and toys lined up on every piece of furniture in the room, and Susan couldn't yell at her for taking up more than her half of the space.

The first day of school in Lakeview came too fast. We were barely moved in, still living out of boxes and suitcases. Susan had fits trying to find the things she needed for her "first day of school outfit."

"I know the movers must have lost a whole carton of my things," Susan wailed, dumping stuff on the living room floor as she rummaged through boxes of clothes.

Mom was trying to help Liz get ready and didn't seem too pleased about all the confusion. "Don't be so fussy, Susan. Just put on what you can find for today. And don't leave those things on the floor."

"Mother, you don't understand. The impression I create today could make or break my whole year. It's really terribly important."

Susan ran back upstairs with an armload of clothes. Liz was standing on one foot, then the other, as Mom tried to brush through her thick curly hair. Liz was the only one in the family with red hair, and she hated it. "Liz, you have to stand still, or I can't do this."

"I don't feel good, Mommy. My tummy aches and I think I'm going to throw up."

"It's just nerves, honey. You'll be fine as soon as you meet the other children. It's always hard going into a new situation."

"I don't want to go. I don't even remember how to get to my school. Please, can Ben take me?"

"Ben has to catch a school bus to get to the high school."

I was all ready for school and just killing time. "I can walk her over to her school and still get back in time for my bus, Mom."

Mom looked relieved. "If you're sure it won't make you late, Ben, that would be wonderful." Mom gave us each a bag lunch and a hug. "Goodbye, you two. I should be home from work before school is out, so I'll be waiting to hear how the first day went for you both."

We headed out the front door, Liz clinging to my hand. There were quite a few kids about Liz's age walking toward the school. I tried to point that out to her, but she just clutched my hand tighter and wouldn't take her eyes off the sidewalk. "You'd better watch how we get to school so you can find your way home this afternoon."

She looked up at me, her eyes round with fear. "Aren't you coming to get me, Ben?"

"I can't, Liz. Your school lets out almost an hour before mine does. Besides, I have to take a school bus, and that might make me even later."

Liz's lower lip began to tremble and I thought she was going to cry. We had arrived at the corner of the main street and a stern-looking crossing guard in a navy blue uniform held out her arms, making us wait. Within a few seconds, we were surrounded by a whole group of kids, all chattering with each other. I felt kind of stupid, towering above everybody, especially since the crossing guard was giving me the once-over. She probably thought I was some dumb kid who had been left back a lot. I saw Liz eyeing the other kids from under her long lashes. As she pushed closer to my side, I could feel her shaking.

We finally arrived at her school. "Okay, Liz, you can do it from here. Give your card to that lady at the door and she'll help you find your class."

"Don't leave me, Ben. I can't go in. I'll never find my way home."

"Sure you will. What's your new address?"

"Twenty-five Summerville Drive."

"Just tell that to the crossing guard and she'll head you in the right direction."

"She looked mean."

"Come on, Liz. You're being silly." That was the wrong thing to say. A big tear started down her cheek. I changed my tactics and put my hands on her shoulders. "Hey, listen. Do you remember that book you had about Homer the Homing Pigeon?"

"Yes, but . . ."

"Just pretend you're Homer. He could find his way home from anywhere in the whole world, right?"

"I guess so."

"Sure he could. So you can at least find your way home from a few blocks away, can't you?"

"Well, I don't know. I . . ."

"Aren't you smarter than a pigeon?"

Liz was starting to smile. "Ben, you're silly."

"Silly, nothing! Do you know how small the brain of a pigeon is? It's about the size of a marble. No sister of mine has a pigeon-sized brain, except maybe Susan."

Liz giggled right out loud at that one, and I knew she was going to be okay. She hugged me. "Oh, Ben, I love you."

"Me too, squirt. Now get in there before you make us both late. I'll see you at home this afternoon and we'll go exploring or something, okay?"

"Can we go to the little stone village where they play golf?"

"Anything you want."

"I can't wait. See you later."

She turned and skipped down the sidewalk to the lady at the door. I saw the lady introduce her to another little girl, and they went into the school together.

I turned and headed back to the main street where we were supposed to catch the school bus. I could see a bunch of kids in the distance, but there wasn't any sign of a bus, so I slowed down. I didn't want to wait at the bus stop with a bunch of kids I didn't know. Worse yet, I didn't want to wait with Susan.

While I was trying to make things easier for Liz, I'd forgotten to worry about my own first day of school. Now all the fears that had been gnawing at the edge of my stomach came back full force. I thought I was going to be sick. I couldn't stand the thought of having to start making friends all over again. It had taken me all of kindergarten and half of first grade to make friends with

Herbie. I'd probably be lucky if I found a friend in Lakeview before I graduated from high school.

The school bus arrived and I ran to catch it just as everybody crowded in. I found a seat way in the back and stared out the window. The bus got noisier at each stop as more kids found people they hadn't seen all summer. I just sat there like a lump in the middle of all the activity.

The bus left our neighborhood and went through a real fancy area with big houses set back from the road by long curved driveways. There weren't many kids from this section, so only one got on at each stop. I noticed one of them sat down in the empty seat next to Susan.

I hadn't been watching where we were going, and now we were passing a busy shopping center. The road widened into six lanes with a center divider, like an expressway. We turned off the next exit, into a big parking lot behind a whole row of buses, and I saw my new school for the first time. It was huge and ugly and looked just like a prison, but without the barbed wire.

I let myself be carried along with the crowd as we moved off the bus. Susan was way up ahead, chattering with three other girls. I reached in my back pocket and pulled out the school registration card that had been mailed to us. It said I was supposed to report to room 157 for homeroom.

I stopped just inside the front door to get my bearings. This was the biggest school I'd ever seen. One hall went straight back from the main entrance and two others branched off to the right and left. I wasn't sure which way to go. I chose the middle hall, where the numbers started at 100 and went up.

The last room on that hall was only 134, so I had to turn around. It was harder trying to get back to the main entrance because everybody was coming toward me. I moved way over to one side, but people were still bumping into me, walking in threes and fours. They were all so busy talking to each other, they didn't even notice me. I caught little pieces of conversation as I tried to push through the crowds.

"We spent the first part of the summer at the Cape. You'll never guess who was . . ."

"Frankie broke his nose playing baseball. They had to . . ."

"You're kidding, Rhonda. I don't believe you really . . ."

"Wait till you see the new math teacher. He looks just like Paul Newman only he has . . ."

Finally I made it back to the front entrance. The hallway to the right started with 135, so it seemed as if I was on the right track.

The crowds were thinning out now and I walked faster because I figured the first bell would be ringing any minute. I passed room 150. Getting warm. All of a sudden, the hall ended at 154. Rats! I'd made the wrong choice again. Just as I turned to go back down the hall, the bell jangled, and I nearly jumped out of my skin. The last few stragglers disappeared into doorways along the hall.

I ran back to the main entrance, my footsteps echoing in the empty hall. I could feel the sweat starting to run down under my arms. Now I was going to have to walk in late and make a big scene. I'd planned to fade into the woodwork and not make any waves in this new school.

I started down the left hall, but the first room was 160. That was impossible! There were five rooms missing on this floor and one of them was my homeroom! The halls were completely empty now. I felt stupid just standing there, so I ducked out the front door. I was trying to figure out what to do next when a big guy in a uniform stepped out from behind some bushes.

"It's a little early to start skipping class, isn't it, kid? Couldn't you at least wait until first period?"

I didn't want to admit I'd been too stupid to find my class, so I just looked down at my feet and kicked at some stones in the dirt.

"Oh, so you're the strong silent type, are you? Maybe you'd better come with me."

I followed him back into the school. He led me to an office and told me to sit on the bench right outside the door marked PRINCIPAL. There were a couple of other kids already on the bench, but they didn't pay any attention when I sat down. A secretary looked up from her typing and glared at me. I felt like a jerk.

Pretty soon the door opened and the principal came out. He seemed to be built out of squares, with broad shoulders and a massive jaw. Even in his suit and vest, you could see he was all muscle. He spoke in a soft voice and didn't try to act tough, but I could tell this principal was someone you wouldn't want to mess with.

"Well, the sweep tells me I have my first visitors of the school year." His eyes scanned down the bench, stopping for a few seconds when he got to me, then moving on. "I'm sure you boys didn't intend to cut class on the very first day, did you?"

The other guys mumbled without looking up.

"No, sir."

"No, Mr. Ramsey."

"You know our policy about sweeping the halls and school grounds after each class bell has sounded."

More mumbling.

"Yeah."

"Yes, sir."

"I expect my students to be in their proper classrooms, not hanging around. Is that clear?"

The bell rang, which covered up what the other kids were answering. I couldn't quite hear, but it sounded like one of them had said something a little heavier than "Yes, sir."

Whatever it was, Mr. Ramsey hadn't heard it. "All right, kids. I'm letting this one pass, but I don't want any more trouble from any of you. Get going to your first period classes."

We all got up and went into the hall. The other two guys disappeared into classrooms as soon as we were around the corner. Now I was really in a mess. I didn't have any idea where my classes were. All I'd been given was a homeroom number, and I hadn't even been able to find that. I decided to make one more try down the hall that ended in 154. Maybe I'd overlooked something before, because I was rushing.

Sure enough, when I got to the end of the hall there was a little hall that turned off to the right with a few rooms on it, and one of them was 157. A big crowd of kids was bunched up at the door. They all looked pretty old, at least high school age. I could see the teacher sitting at her desk, but by the time I made my way through to her, the bell was ringing. She looked up at me over her glasses. "You must be in the wrong room. This is French four, all seniors." Then she stood up. "Je vous souhaite la bienvenue. Cette année . . ."

I could see she wasn't going to be any help, so I mumbled something about being sorry and backed out of the room. Nobody even noticed. I just stood there in the hall for a few minutes. School had always been hard for me, but in this place I couldn't even figure out where I was supposed to go. The only thing I could do was sneak out and try again tomorrow. At least now I knew where my homeroom was. All I needed was a fresh start. If I got home the same time as the bus, nobody would know anything was wrong. I just hoped Susan would be busy enough with her new friends not to notice that I wasn't there. Susan had spent her whole life trying to catch me messing up, and she usually succeeded.

I started feeling a little better. There was a door at the end of the short hallway, so I slipped out and started across the parking lot. All of a sudden, a hand came down on my shoulder. "Not so fast, kid. Where do you think you're . . . well, I'll be."

I turned around to face "the sweep," the big guy in the uniform. "You sure are doing your best to get in trouble, aren't you?"

I couldn't say anything. I just put my head down and let him lead me back into school. I didn't have anything to say to Mr. Ramsey when he questioned me either.

"What's your name, son?"

"Ben." My voice barely came out.

"So, Ben. You seem to be having trouble staying in class."

I was thinking I wouldn't have any trouble staying in class if I could just find it in the first place, but I didn't say that. I just looked down at the floor.

"What's your full name, Ben?"

I cleared my throat. "Ben . . . Benjamin Wagner."

"All right, Benjamin Wagner, wait right here." Mr. Ramsey went out into the main office, came back thumbing through a folder with my name on it, and sat down at his desk. He read for a few minutes, then tilted back in his chair, his arms folded across his chest. "Ben, this says you just moved up here from the southern tier. Phillipsburg, is that right?"

"Yes, sir."

"Maybe they did things differently where you came from, Ben, but here we expect our students to be in their assigned classrooms. Is that understood?"

"Yes, sir."

He leaned forward on his elbows and looked right at me. "Ben, I can't ignore the fact that you were caught cutting class twice in one morning. I'm going to have to call your parents. I want to turn you around before things get out of hand. Do you understand?"

I nodded. I could just imagine my father's reaction to this. I'd probably be grounded for a year.

Another bell jangled in the hall outside Mr. Ramsey's office. He looked up at the clock. "Well, you might as well get back to class. Where are you supposed to be second period?"

I didn't have any idea so I just shrugged.

"Did you lose your schedule already?"

I nodded.

Mr. Ramsey was losing patience. "I'm trying to give you the benefit of the doubt, Ben, but you're not making it easy for me. You're going to have to improve your attitude." He pulled a paper out of my folder. "Here's an extra copy of your schedule. You have social studies now with Mr. Beekman. He's in room 167. Do you know where that is?"

"No, sir."

Mr. Ramsey took me into the hall. "It's down that way, fourth room on the right. Now, get going. I don't want to see you in here again."

"Yes, sir. Thank you, sir." I pocketed the schedule and headed down the hall. At least for now, I knew where to go, but I had the feeling it was too late. So much for a fresh start.

Somehow I got through the rest of the school day

without any more problems. I wasn't used to changing rooms after each class, but I managed to find my way around. Lunch was a drag because I didn't know anybody, so I just went and sat alone at a table in the far corner. At least I wasn't getting yelled at for anything. The worst part would be having to face my parents at the end of the day, especially Dad.

I could see Susan a few tables away from me. She was sitting with some girls I recognized from the school bus, the ones from the rich section. Susan could smell money a mile away. She must have sensed I was watching her because she looked up. Next thing I knew, she was heading my way.

"Hi, little brother. I see your social life is jumping as usual. Do you suppose all your new little friends here could move over and let me sit down to chat with you for a minute?" She slithered into the chair across the table from me.

"Never mind the jokes, Susan. I like eating alone. It gives me time to think."

"Oh, he needs time to think, now," she said to an imaginary person in the chair next to her. "We must all be very quiet so we don't disturb him. Ben isn't used to thinking, you know, so the dear boy needs all the practice he can get."

"Knock it off, Susan."

"Poor Ben," she cooed. "You're just lost without your little playmate, aren't you? Too bad you couldn't have dragged Herbie along to Lakeview, like a security blanket."

"Susan, get the heck out of here, or I'll . . ."

"You'll what, little brother?" I didn't have an answer to her challenge. No matter how mad I got at Susan, I knew there was nothing I could do to her that wouldn't just get me in more trouble. There were times, though, when it almost seemed worth risking the punishment just to belt her right in that big mouth of hers.

Satisfied by my silence, she got right down to business. "I need five dollars, little brother."

"So go rob a bank."

"I know you have that much. You always save your allowance."

"Even if I did have that much money, I wouldn't let you get at it."

Susan's eyes narrowed. She was moving in for the kill. "Mom and Dad should be especially interested," she hissed, "in the fact that you were sent to the principal's office twice in one morning, your very first morning in this school." She sat back in her seat and started examining her long, red fingernails. "Now, if you were willing to give me that five dollars I asked for, I probably could manage a lapse of memory about the whole incident."

I should have known Susan would find out about me. Every time I'd ever messed up in my whole life, Susan had managed to be right there to see it. Then she'd blackmail me and threaten to squeal to Mom and Dad if I didn't pay up. This time I'd given her enough ammunition to last for months.

I was just about to cough up the money when a thought struck me. There was no way I could cover up what had happened this morning because the principal was going to call Mom and Dad. I suddenly realized I was off the hook, and I started to laugh.

That really spooked Susan. She must have thought she'd pushed me over the edge and I was going nuts. "What . . . what's so funny?"

"No deal, Susan," I said. "The principal has already called Mom and Dad by now, so what happened isn't any deep dark secret. Your days of blackmailing are over. Go find yourself another sucker." No cover-up, no blackmail. I was free!

Susan pushed back from the table abruptly. "Maybe you wriggled out of this one, but I'll get you sooner or later."

In spite of Susan's parting threat, I felt great for the rest of the day, right up until the time I got off the bus. My victory over her had made me forget about the battle I'd be facing at home.

4

Mom was unpacking dishes and putting them away in the kitchen cupboard when I walked in. Liz was home too, pigging out on Oreos and talking with her mouth full.

". . . and then Mrs. Reynolds had us each draw a picture of our favorite things to do, so I did one of me racing against Mario Andretti in my Swan Lake costume and she said it was very imaginative and put it up on the bulletin board with some of the other . . . Oh, Ben!" Liz jumped up when she noticed me, almost tipping over her glass of milk. "School was wonderful! I have three new friends already and they all live right around here. You were right about Lakeview, Ben. It's going to be just fine. I don't hardly even miss Phillipsburg anymore."

As Liz hugged me I looked over at Mom. The expression on Mom's face told me that the principal had called her. I turned my attention back to Liz. "Hey, that's great, Liz. Really had a good day, huh?"

"It was terrific. We even had an assembly and they showed a movie about horses. Then at recess we went out on the playground. They had this neat thing to climb on that looked like a ship, with a mast, and big fishing nets, and a captain's wheel and everything." She stopped to take a breath and looked up at me. "Did you have a good day too, Ben?"

"Oh, yeah. Great." I looked over and saw the muscles around Mom's jaw get tight, so I figured I'd better change the subject. "Hey, Liz, let's go over to see that stone village. Want to?"

Liz was stuffing the last bit of cookie into her mouth. "I can't, Ben," she said, licking the crumbs off her fingers. "Two of my new friends, Lisa and Jennifer, are coming over to play. I have to unpack my Barbie stuff." She turned back, just as she reached the stairs. "Can we go to the stone village some other time?"

"Anytime, Liz. You name it."

There was an uncomfortable silence after Liz left the room. I cleared my throat. "Sounds like Liz got along pretty well today."

Mom's eyes looked sad and tired. "Do you mind telling me what got into that head of yours at school this morning?"

"It was all a mistake, Mom," I mumbled, looking at the floor.

36

"A mistake! Ben, I just can't believe you'd start out this way in a new school. Your father is furious. When I told him about the call from the principal, he was so angry, I had all I could do to keep him from going over to that school and dragging you home. I just hope you have a good explanation for all this."

"It was all a big mix-up, Mom. I couldn't find my homeroom, and then the bell rang for the first class. I went outside and then this big guy with a radio picked me up and . . ."

I was interrupted by a knock at the back door. Mom went to answer it. "You must be Liz's new friends," she said, letting the two little girls into the kitchen. The skinny one with two teeth missing spoke up. "We came to take Elithabeth to my houth to play dollth. I'm Litha."

Mom smiled. "Why don't you sit down and each have a cookie. I'll tell Liz to hurry up."

I took the interruption as a chance to escape. I really wasn't in the mood to talk about my day anyway. "I'm going out to look around town, Mom."

"But we didn't finish . . ." Mom looked down at the two little kids who were carefully separating the two sides of their Oreos so they could eat the frosting first. Lisa was having a hard time scraping off the frosting with her teeth because the missing ones left a ridge of frosting on the cookie. Mom started to laugh, then caught herself and turned back to me. "Go ahead for now, Ben, but for heaven's sake be home on time for dinner. Your father wants to eat at five o'clock sharp."

"Okay, Mom." I bolted out the door and headed toward

the lake. I had to pass Dad's barbershop to get there, but I stayed on the opposite side of the road. I could see Dad and Mr. Romano in there, each doing a haircut. Dad was laughing, looking real happy. At least this time I could just tell him the truth about what happened, without Susan messing me up. I didn't have anything to feel guilty about, because I hadn't done anything wrong. Stupid, maybe, but not wrong. I almost thought about going into the barbershop to talk to Dad while he was in such a good mood, but decided it would be better to wait until he got home.

I kept going down the road, climbed up the bank, and was stunned all over again by the size of the lake. It seemed as if you could see the curve of the earth on the horizon line.

I walked along the shoreline and automatically started looking for skipping stones, like Herbie and I always did at the crick in Phillipsburg. It was harder to find good flat stones here. Most of them were round, almost egg shaped. I found a couple of good ones and lobbed them at the lake, but the waves threw my timing off and they sank after one or two skips.

A picture of Herbie and me skipping stones at the crick, flashed through my mind. Where was I going to find another Herbie in Lakeview? This new place seemed so strange to me. I needed a friend now, more than I ever had in my whole life.

Suddenly, a stone zinged over my shoulder, took four skips, jumped over the crest of a wave, and skipped three more times on the other side before it sank. Wow!

"Herbie?" The name slipped out of my mouth as I whirled around to see who had thrown the stone. I almost dropped my teeth when I looked behind me. It was a girl, a skinny, black-haired, knobby-kneed girl!

We stared at each other for a couple of seconds. Then she reached in the pocket of her cut-off jeans and pulled out another stone. She never took her eyes off me as she wound up. Zing! The thing went past me like a bullet. I turned to watch it skim over the surface until just before the crest of the next wave. Then it jumped like a porpoise, did four more skips on the other side of the wave, and seemed to float on the surface for a few seconds before it sank.

Girl or not, that was a great skip! I looked over my shoulder to tell her so, but she was gone. Then I saw her farther down the beach, running.

"Hey! Wait a minute," I called.

She turned and paused for a second, and I started out after her. Then she smiled and started running again, disappearing behind a point that jutted out over the beach. I ran past the point, expecting to see her on the other side, but the beach was empty, except for a mangy black dog sniffing a dead fish at the water's edge. The dog looked up, startled, and ran off.

Past the point, the land dropped down to water level and had houses on it. Well, not houses, exactly. They were more like little shacks, packed in close together and leaning on each other for support. There was another row of old buildings on the other side of the road, and behind them, the bay. The strip of land, just wide enough to hold the road, two rows of shacks, and a narrow beach, was like a dam, keeping the lake from coming into the bay. I poked around for a while, but the place was starting to give me the creeps. Wherever the girl had gone, she wasn't going to let me find her, so I gave up and started for home.

I walked along the edge of the bay for a little while, then found a path that cut back up toward the main road. A pier lined with fishermen jutted out over the bay. I wanted to go see what kind of fish they were pulling in, but decided I'd better wait until I had more time. Oh my gosh — time! I'd completely forgotten about being back at five o'clock.

I reached the main road and backtracked to peek in the window of the barbershop. It was closed and the clock said 5:20. I was really in for it now!

I sprinted all the way back to our house and tried to slip through the front door without being heard. Maybe I could sneak up to my room and pretend I'd been there all along.

A roar came from the kitchen. "Ben? That you?"

"Yes, sir," I said, one foot already on the stairs.

"Get in here, pronto."

I moved into the kitchen doorway. The rest of the family was sitting around the table finishing up dinner. The smell of meatloaf suddenly reminded me how hungry I was, so I went in and started to pull out my chair.

Dad hooked the chair leg with his foot. "So you think you're going to waltz in here thirty minutes late and help yourself to a meal, do you?"

"I'm sorry. I didn't notice the time."

"Didn't notice, huh? Well, I noticed!"

Liz had slid down in her seat, her huge eyes watching me over a mound of mashed potatoes. Susan was looking down at her plate, trying not to show how much she was enjoying the whole scene.

"Get up to your room," Dad yelled.

Mom reached over and touched Dad's arm. "George, couldn't he at least . . ."

"Get! Up! To! Your! Room!" Dad bellowed, in a voice that could've been heard over a rock concert.

I hit the stairs before he finished his sentence. I had the feeling I'd reached new heights of getting into trouble. Stretching out on my bed, I waited for Dad to come up and lower the boom.

I kept thinking about the girl on the beach, the way she seemed to appear out of nowhere, and disappear the same way. There was something strange about her, but she sure was the best stone skipper I'd ever seen. I wished Herbie could've seen her flip one over the wave like that. I was just thinking I should get up and write to Herbie and tell him about it, when I heard footsteps thundering up the stairs.

Dad appeared in the doorway and stood there glaring at me. I sat up on the edge of my bed, almost wishing he'd just give me a good belt and get it over with fast, instead of making such a big deal out of everything.

"I'm waiting to hear your explanation of what went on in school today."

My mind was racing, trying to find the right words to make Dad see what had happened. "It wasn't the way it looked, Dad."

Dad's face looked like a storm cloud as he came toward me. "Oh no? Just how was it then?"

I usually couldn't manage to say anything to Dad, especially when he was really mad, but I had to make him understand this time. My words all tumbled out on top of each other. "Well, I couldn't find my homeroom because the halls were numbered funny and I didn't see this little hall that went off to the side. That's where my homeroom was, but I didn't know it, because I was trying to hurry, I guess . . . and then the bell rang, which I was afraid it was going to do . . . and everybody went into their classrooms and I didn't know where I was supposed to be, so I went out the front door and . . ."

"Ben!" Dad barked out my name in the same tone of voice he would have yelled "Ten-HUT!" in the Marines. "The truth!"

"But this is the truth, sir."

"Oh, yeah? Well, if you didn't knew where your homeroom was," he said, leaning forward until his face was close to mine, "why didn't you *ask* someone?"

I knew Dad wouldn't understand how lost I'd felt, or how I couldn't ask for directions. If this had happened to Dad when he was a kid, he would've stood in the middle of the hall with a big smile and yelled, "Where the heck did they hide room 157?" and about forty-five kids would have run up to lead him to his homeroom. That was the difference between Dad and me.

"Well, I'm waiting. Do you have an explanation?"

I just shook my head.

"What? I can't hear you."

"No, sir." Geez! I was back to my usual answer, the one I used when I was guilty.

Dad pulled the chair out from my desk and sat down with a disgusted look on his face. "You know, Ben. If you'd told me the truth, I might have been more lenient with you. But you had to make up some cockeyed story about not being able to find your homeroom."

Why wouldn't he believe me? I kept my head down, because I could feel tears starting to sting my eyes, and I couldn't let him think I was crying. Being a sissy was even worse than being a liar in Dad's book. Only girls were allowed to cry.

"You know, Susan tried to bail you out of this mess by sticking up for you, and if you had told things to me the way they really happened, I might have seen it your way. Susan told me about those kids who called you a hick and said you were too much of a sissy to cut your classes. She thought you did it only to show you weren't afraid of them."

So that was it. Good old Susan got to Dad before I did. She made up some kind of story so Dad would think she was sticking up for me. No wonder I couldn't win against Susan. She could twist things around in so many directions, I didn't know which way was up.

Dad was still yelling at me. "Can you give me any reason why you shouldn't be punished for cutting class and then lying about the whole thing?"

The way he made it sound, I felt like I was on my way to the electric chair. At least a condemned man got to choose his last meal. I didn't even get a last meal! Dad launched into a big lecture about responsibility and earning trust. I tuned him out and tried to look as if I was listening. I couldn't stand it when Dad went on and on like that. He always made me feel like a worm. I tuned back in just in time to hear him deliver my sentence.

"Now, for the next two weeks of school days, you're grounded. But instead of wasting time sitting in your room, I want you to come to the barbershop each day, as soon as you get off the school bus. You can clean up, wait on customers, and just generally make yourself useful. You'll come home with me for dinner, then up here to your room to do your homework. Is that clear?"

"Yes, sir."

"I expect good grades out of you this year, Ben. There's no reason why you shouldn't bring home report cards as good as Susan's. I don't like being this tough on you, but you're going to straighten up, or else."

"Yes, sir."

I never knew what "or else" meant, but I sure wasn't going to try and find out. Dad left, and I let out a long,

44

slow breath. The two weeks weren't going to be much fun, but at least the speech was over. That was one good thing about Dad. He'd tell you something once, and he wouldn't repeat it unless you screwed up again. I wasn't planning on screwing up, if I could help it.

I was lying on my bed, listening to my stomach growl, when there was a little tap at the door. "Ben, let me in." It was Liz.

"Come on in, squirt. It's not locked."

"I can't. Hurry, Ben."

When I opened the door, Liz rushed in carrying a plate with meatloaf and potatoes drenched in gravy in one hand, and a glass of milk in the other. A double stream of milk and gravy followed her into the room.

"Hold it, Liz. You're leaving a trail here."

She plopped the plate and glass down on my desk, spilling some more gravy. "I'm sorry, Ben. I'm not good at climbing and holding things at the same time."

I grabbed an old T-shirt and mopped up the evidence on the stairs and floor. "No problem. It's all cleaned up. Let me at the feast."

"It may be a little cold. I had to hide in the hall closet with it until Dad left."

"That's okay. A starving man doesn't mind eating cold meatloaf." I made a mental note to check the hall closet for gravy puddles after Liz left.

Liz climbed up on my bed and sat cross-legged, watching me eat. She looked as if she wanted to say something, but couldn't get it out.

"What's the matter, Liz?" I asked, taking a big gulp of milk to make the stiff, cold potatoes slide down my throat.

"Nothing. I just . . . Did you do something terrible at school, Ben?"

"Not really, but it looked that way to other people."

"I knew you wouldn't do anything bad on purpose. It just happened, right?"

"Yeah, that's about it, I guess."

Liz looked solemn. "I know how that is. It happens to me all the time. I don't mean to do anything bad, but all of a sudden . . . well, it just happens, that's all."

"Yeah, I know what you mean, Liz."

"And the worst part is, Susan is always there to see it."

"That's for sure. Susan Super-sleuth."

Liz giggled at that, then got serious again. "Ben, you want to know something awful?"

"Sure. What?"

"I think I hate Susan. Is it a terrible thing, to hate your own sister?"

"No, in Susan's case I think it's pretty reasonable."

"Good! That's what I thought." She got up off the bed to go mess around with my model plane collection.

I polished off the last of the meal, then helped Liz load the stuff to sneak back downstairs. "See you tomorrow, Ben."

"Thanks, Liz. You saved my life."

I watched her pick her way down the stairs, like a tightrope walker in a circus act. Good old Liz. At least someone in this family understood me.

About a half hour later, there was another knock at the door.

"Ben?" It was Mom.

"Yeah, Mom, come on in."

"Get the door, will you? My hands are full."

When I opened the door, Mom came into the room with a sandwich and a glass of milk and set them down on my desk.

"I couldn't let you go without supper, Ben. Eat this up now, so I can take the dishes back down."

I wasn't sure I could find room for any more food, but I didn't want to give Liz away by saying I'd already eaten. "Gee, thanks, Mom. You didn't have to do this."

"I couldn't let you go to bed hungry, Ben."

"Dad really threw the book at me this time," I said. I took a bite of the sandwich. It was cold meatloaf.

"It was the lying that got to him. He might have understood how you could make a mistake, but he won't tolerate lies."

"I just can't make him understand, Mom. I tried, but he won't listen. Susan's the one who's lying."

"Now wait a minute, Ben. Your sister did her best to smooth things over for you. She tried to make your father see that you weren't entirely at fault, but then you came up with that ridiculous story. I don't blame your father for being angry."

"He's always angry where I'm concerned. Susan never does anything wrong around here, does she? I bet if Susan murdered somebody, Dad would find excuses for her, and you'd go along with him."

"You're not being fair, Ben. I know Susan's not as perfect as she'd like us to believe, but she did stick up for you today, and I don't think I've ever seen you do the same for her."

I could see that I wasn't going to get anywhere with Mom, so I concentrated on shoving down the last of the sandwich and vowed I'd never eat meatloaf again.

*

The minute I opened my eyes the next morning, I thought of the stone skipper. I had to see her again and, since I'd be grounded during the week, my only hope was to see her in school. I started working out a plan in my mind as I got dressed. The school bus would have to go past the shacks before it got to our neighborhood, so she'd already be on the bus when it got to our stop. I couldn't risk looking around while I was on the bus, because Susan might start getting nosy. The less she knew about my business, the better. Instead, I'd sit right in the front so I could be the first one off. Then I could hang around next to the door and watch the rest of the kids get off. I'd only seen the stone skipper's face for a few seconds, but I knew I could recognize her from that black, wavy hair.

When the bus arrived, I managed to slip into the seat right opposite the driver. I knew that the stone skipper must be sitting somewhere behind me, and that made the bus trip seem endless. I could almost feel her eyes on the back of my neck. As soon as the bus pulled to a stop, I jumped out and stood near the door, watching the kids pile off. She must have sat way in the back. My heart was pounding in my throat. Where was she? What would I say to her when she got off? I could see that the last girl in line had dark hair. Maybe if she didn't recognize me, I could just follow her to see where her homeroom was.

I took a deep breath when the dark-haired girl came down the steps, then breathed out with a puff. It wasn't her at all. This girl wasn't the stone skipper, and she looked annoyed to see me staring at her. I turned and tried to catch up with the line of kids from our bus, but they were all mixed in with streams of kids from other buses. How could I have missed her?

At the end of the day, I posted myself outside the front door where I could watch everyone getting on our bus. I waited until the last second before I got on, but the stone skipper never showed up.

I headed straight for the barbershop when I got off. Mr. Romano greeted me with a big smile.

"So, Ben. You're going to help out with the business, eh? You'll make a fine barber some day. Go help yourself to a candy bar."

Dad wasn't quite so friendly. "He's here to work and get himself straightened out, Angie. He can forget about the candy."

Mr. Romano shrugged and smiled at me. I knew he liked me. He had a whole bunch of his own kids, most of them grown up now. I think he was disappointed that none of them wanted to take over the barbershop. Even though the shop belonged to Dad now, Mr. Romano had agreed to stay on for a couple of months and help Dad get to know the customers.

Dad handed me the broom. "You can start by sweeping up."

I took the broom and started pushing tufts of hair into a big pile. There were all colors — brown, blond, red, and even a blue-black like the stone skipper's hair.

My next job was to check out the magazine shipment. Mr. Romano showed me how to do it. The new magazines were packed in big bundles fastened with a heavy wire that had to be cut with pliers. Then there was a long list on top of each bundle, called an invoice. I had to find each magazine by name, make sure we had the right number, and make a big check mark on the list with a red pencil. Then I put the new issues on the shelf and took the old ones off to be sent back to the company for credit.

I finished up before it was time to go and Dad didn't have any more work for me, so I took a comic book and sat in the waiting area by the window. I could barely see the curve in the road leading to the place where all the shacks were. I really wanted to know more about those shacks and who lived in them. I went over to Mr. Romano, who was cleaning a bunch of combs in the sink. Dad was finishing up a haircut and was busy talking to the man in his chair.

"Mr. Romano?"

"Yes, Ben? What can I do for you?"

"What's that strip of land that goes between the bay and the lake? Does anybody live in those old shacks?"

"You mean the sandbar? You haven't been hanging around out there, have you?"

"No, I saw it while I was doing some exploring. I just wondered about it, that's all."

"That's a good place to stay away from, Ben. The people who live out there are squatters, built those miserable shacks on land that doesn't even belong to them. Most of the shacks have been there for years, although I don't know what keeps them standing. Anyway, it's a rough bunch of people on that sandbar. There's even a legend that a family of witches has lived out there for generations."

"No kidding. Have you ever seen them? Do people around here really believe in that stuff, about witches, I mean?"

"I don't know, Ben. They say legends are usually based on some truth. I wouldn't go looking for witches on that sandbar if I were you. You might find more trouble than you bargained for."

As I headed for home, I kept thinking about what Mr. Romano had said. I wondered if a real witch would look like the ones you see at Halloween, or would she be disguised as a normal person? If there were witches living on the sandbar, did the stone skipper know about them? I mulled it over in my mind for a few minutes, then I came back to my senses. This was stupid. I was letting my imagination run wild. Everyone knew witches were just make-believe.

5

I watched for the stone skipper all week, on the bus and in school, but I didn't have any luck finding her. I also didn't have any luck making new friends, which didn't surprise me. I'd never been a whiz in the social department.

At least working at the barbershop kept my mind off being lonesome. I was too busy to even think about it during the week. I was only grounded on school nights, so on Saturday I was free to go look for the stone skipper.

I was the first one up Saturday morning and made myself a quick breakfast of cold cereal. I bounded out of the house, but had to run back up to my room to get a sweat shirt because it was pretty cold out. Fall was coming on fast. The sun came out for only a few minutes at a time from behind huge gray clouds, and a brisk wind was stirring up whitecaps on the lake. The only people out at that hour were some joggers and, after a while, an old man who came to feed hunks of bread to the sea gulls. I stayed to watch the slow circling of the gulls for a while, then moved on down the beach, away from the sandbar.

I could see a lighthouse in the distance, at the end of a long pier, and started hiking toward it until the mouth of a wide creek kept me from going any farther. Turning back toward the Lakeview beach, I hoped the stone skipper had come out while I was walking in the other direction, but the beach was deserted.

A group of black clouds started bumping into each other where the sky met the water, and pretty soon I could hear thunder rolling around in the distance. It was raining way out toward Canada, with slanting streaks that seemed to anchor the clouds to the lake, but the storm kept moving east along the horizon and never got any closer to shore. I walked all the way back to the point, but after what Mr. Romano had said about the people on the sandbar, I didn't feel like going out there alone. I didn't really believe the part about witches, but the place gave me the creeps anyway.

I gave up the search around noon and went home for lunch. As I came over the bank onto Beach Road, I saw Dad heading for the barbershop, but I hung back so he wouldn't see me. I had had about all of Dad I could handle during the week.

Mom and Susan were unpacking the last of the cartons

as I came in the door. "I didn't think we'd see you for lunch, Ben," Mom said. "The soup's all gone. There's just half a tuna sandwich left."

"That's okay, Mom. I'll eat that and make myself a couple of peanut butter sandwiches."

"Good. I feel like a short order cook today. Everyone's been in and out at different times. You just missed your father."

Liz had a friend over for lunch, and they were all giggly and stupid as they slurped their soup. I hoped this wasn't the beginning of Liz turning into a dippy female like her older sister.

"Oh, no!" Susan cried, digging down into one of the cartons.

"What's wrong, honey?" Mom asked.

Susan held up a piece of blue china. "Look, the movers must have broken Grandma's vase."

Mom reached down in the carton and pulled out some more pieces. "I can't believe it. I thought it was packed so securely."

"Can we glue it back together?" I asked. I knew how much that vase meant to Mom.

Mom shook her head. "I don't think so. There must be a hundred pieces in here. Wouldn't you know they'd break something I really cared about? The dime store china came through without a crack."

Liz nudged her friend Jennifer and they shoved down the last of their sandwiches real fast so they could get back up to Liz's room. Mom sat down at the table with me and we tried moving some of the pieces around like a jigsaw puzzle, but nothing matched.

Susan put her arm around Mom's shoulder. "I don't think that's going to do any good, Mother. Some of those pieces are so tiny we could never put it back together."

Mom pushed back from the table. "I guess you're right, and I'm not going to cry over it, but that moving company is going to hear about this. For now, I'll go out and do the shopping to take my mind off it."

Susan kissed Mom on the cheek. "I'm going out too, Mom. One of my friends over in Willow Point asked me if I could come over this afternoon. Okay?" Leave it to Susan to hook up with the rich kids. She'd probably marry a millionaire someday.

Mom smiled. "Sure, go ahead, Susan. We're just about finished here anyway." Susan made a break for it, letting the screen door slam behind her.

*

Mom ran around trying to find her purse and car keys. She started out the door, then came back in and felt around in the jar she where she stored the grocery money. "Ben, have you been borrowing from my grocery jar? There seems to be ten dollars missing."

"Not me, Mom. Maybe it was Dad."

"You're probably right," she said, heading out again.

By the time I started back toward the beach, the sky had changed again. It was still thick with clouds, but they were a light pinkish color, not black like this morning. Each time the sky changed color the lake seemed to change too. The water was pale now, almost lavender, and the whitecaps were smaller and farther apart.

I found a couple of good skipping stones and tried to make them jump over a wave, but I couldn't even come close. Each time the lake would swell up under the stone after two or three skips and sink it.

I'd tried just about every technique I could think of when all of a sudden it happened again! A stone shot past my neck, so close I could feel the breeze from it. One-two-three-four, up and over, one-two-three and a half! I didn't want to scare her off this time, so I didn't turn around. I just kept facing the lake, throwing stones. Each time she'd answer with another spectacular skip. I could tell by the angle of her shots that she was moving up closer behind me.

When she got close enough that I could hear the clink of stones in her pocket, I turned around. She was right behind me, and when I saw her up close for the first time, I almost stopped breathing.

Her hair was blue-black and shiny, and fell in ringlets around her face; but it was her eyes that made me shiver. They didn't seem to belong with the rest of her at all. They were pale lavender-gray, exactly the color of the lake, and I couldn't make myself look away as she stared at me. Then, suddenly, she broke the spell and started running down the beach toward the sandbar. I wasn't going to let her get away this time. I was only a few feet behind her.

"Wait! Stop! I just want to talk to you for a minute."

She didn't stop, but ran faster, even though she was barefoot and the beach was nothing but stones.

When she reached the point, I was only a few yards behind her. She couldn't get out of my sight this time. I rounded the point and stopped dead in my tracks. She'd disappeared again! There was absolutely no place she could've gone in that short a time. The shacks on the sandbar were too far away and the only other escape would have been straight up the wall of the point — but nobody could climb that fast.

I even looked out over the lake to see if she'd ducked down in the water, but there wasn't a living thing in sight. I just stood there like an idiot, looking from one end of the beach to the other. Suddenly, I felt something brush past my leg. I looked down and saw a cat, a shiny blue-black cat with lavender eyes. I stood frozen as the cat watched me. She held me in her gaze for several seconds, then turned and walked slowly on toward the sandbar.

It took a few minutes for my mind to make the connection. I was usually a pretty sensible person, but things were happening that didn't make any sense at all. Twice I'd chased after this girl, and twice she'd disappeared into thin air — or had she? The eyes of that cat had given me the same chill as hers. The last time she'd disappeared there was a dog — a black dog. Was it possible? Could she change herself into anything she wanted? I was stunned by a sudden thought. Was she one of the witches Mr. Romano had been talking about?

The cat stopped and looked back at me, as if she'd

been listening to my thoughts. This was crazy. I was letting myself believe all kinds of ridiculous things. Just to prove to myself that I was wrong, I walked over to the cat and leaned down to pet her.

"Nice kitty," I said. "You're just a regular, normal cat, aren't you?"

The cat just stared at me for a second. Then her ears flattened against her head and a black paw lashed out with the speed of a switchblade, leaving a jagged red line on my thumb. That did it! This cat was anything but normal. I turned and ran as hard as I could toward home.

6

I watched for the witch in school, but now it was to keep away from her, not to find her. I was so busy trying to avoid her, I went through another week of barely speaking to anybody in school. By then I had a reputation as a loner and nobody even bothered with me. I figured it was just as well. You never knew what kind of person you might get mixed up with in that place.

I met a lot of Dad's customers in the shop and some of them said they had kids my age. A few of the kids came in for haircuts and seemed okay, but nobody wants to meet someone through their parents. At least Dad was letting me wear my hair longer now. That's the trouble with being a barber's son — he always cut my hair real short because he said it would be bad advertising to have me go around with hair hanging down my neck. When we first arrived in Lakeview, I was the only kid in town with ears. That didn't help me any in the adjustment department!

Dad was the one who finally had to adjust. When some of the fathers dragged their kids in for haircuts, he had to learn to trim off just a little bit on the bottom. He said he felt like he was stealing their money just to trim off a half inch, but Mr. Romano convinced him he'd lose customers if he didn't do it that way.

Thursday afternoon, when I was in the back of the shop putting out the new magazines, the bell over the door jangled. Usually I automatically looked up, but this time I was trying to sneak a look inside one of those men's magazines and it had my full concentration. Dad's voice brought me back fast, though, and I dropped the magazine back onto the bundle.

"Ben! Customer up front."

I wasn't sure Dad had seen what I was doing, but I kept my eyes down as I went behind the front counter. Some kid was squatting down, looking at the candy bars in the case.

"I'd like a bag of M&M's, please."

As I reached under the counter to grab the candy, I saw the face peering through the front of the glass case. It was her — the witch! I was frozen in place, and the two of us just squatted there staring at each other over the Milky Ways and Hershey bars.

The door jangled again and a man slapped some coins down on the counter. "Hey kid, you stuck down there or somethin'? I got a bus to catch. Gimme a pack of Marlboros."

I got up, pulled a pack of cigarettes out of its cubbyhole, and rang up the sale. The witch had stood up and was staring at me with those huge, pale eyes. Nobody in the shop seemed to be reacting at all. We were in the same room as a witch and everybody acted as if it was perfectly normal.

I put the candy on the counter and she started reaching a hand toward me, her fingers doubled up into a fist. Oh my gosh! She was going to zap me right there and nobody was even going to notice until it was too late. I wanted to yell something but she kept staring at me, and my throat closed up so I couldn't get any sound out.

"Are you going to take these or not?" She turned her hand over and it was filled with pennies. "Come on, put out your hand. They'll roll all over the place if I put them on the counter."

Was it a trick? I reached for the coins, expecting to feel a shock or something when they touched my hand, but nothing happened. I rang up the sale on the cash register, but I put her pennies in with the five-dollar bills. In case there was anything funny about them, I wanted to be able to tell them apart from the others.

The witch opened up her bag of M&M's and popped a few into her mouth. She held the bag out to me. "Want some?"

I just shook my head.

"You probably can get as much candy as you want, huh?"

I really didn't want to talk to her, but she didn't seem in any hurry to leave. "No. I usually have to pay for it like everybody else."

"Oh. Still, it must be nice. You can read the comics and stuff, can't you?"

I could feel my face getting red as I remembered the magazine I'd been looking at. "Well, yeah, but I can't let them get messed up, or I have to pay for them, too."

She looked around. "This is a nice place. I wouldn't mind working in a shop like this. You just moved here, didn't you?" she asked.

"Yeah."

"Where from?" This girl was acting so normal, you'd never suspect she was a witch.

"Phillipsburg. It's down in the southern tier, south of Buffalo."

"Really?" She looked interested. "Did you ever see Lake Erie?"

"No, we were a long way from Buffalo. I just mentioned it because most people have heard of it, and nobody's ever heard of Phillipsburg."

"You're right. I never heard of it." She smiled. It seemed so good to be talking with someone my own age, I was beginning to wonder if I'd been wrong about this witch thing.

"I saw you skipping stones at the lake," she said. "Not

many kids around here know how to do that. Did you have a lake in Phillipsburg?"

"No. Me and my friend Herbie used to hang around the crick a lot. That's where I learned."

She looked puzzled. "What's the crick?"

"A creek, Frew Run Creek is its real name. Everybody just calls it the crick. It's a lot different skipping stones in the lake, though, with the waves and all. You're really good, the way you make the stone jump over the waves."

"I've had a lot of practice. I've always lived on the shore of one of the Great Lakes, mostly this one."

"Do you suppose you could teach me how to do that thing where you flip the stone over a wave?" I asked.

"I guess so. It took me a long time to learn it, though."

"That's okay. I have plenty of time. Will you be at the beach on Saturday?"

"Sure. I'm always there."

"Maybe I'll see you at school before then," I said. "I'm in seventh grade at Westshore. How about you?"

"I'm in seventh grade too, but I go to Crestview, on the other side of the bay. That's because I live out on the sandbar. It's in a different school district."

I looked over at Mr. Romano to see if he'd heard that, but he was talking to his customer. The girl stuffed the bag of M&M's into her pocket and headed for the door.

"Hey, I forgot to ask," I said. "What's your name?"

She turned back and smiled. "It's Regina. Regina St. Clair."

63

"I'm Ben Wagner."

"I'll see you Saturday, Ben Wagner," she said, as she slipped out the door.

I went back to my post at the magazine rack. I knew I was going to have a friend again. I didn't care if she was a girl and a witch. She was somebody to talk to and hang around with. And she was one heck of a good stone skipper, even better than Herbie.

7

Saturday morning dawned bright and clear. I was humming to myself as I whipped up some eggs for French toast. Liz wandered into the kitchen yawning and rubbing one eye, wearing an old pair of fuzzy red sleepers with the feet cut out.

"Hey, squirt. What're you doing up so early?"

"Our Brownie troop is having a cookout for lunch out at Hamlin Beach. I have to get my stuff ready to take."

"Yeah? What're you going to cook?"

"Something with macaroni. We have to cook it on the bottoms of big tin cans."

"What do they have against regular pots and pans?"

"They want us to learn how to survive, in case we ever get lost in the wilderness or something."

"Well, that makes sense. I wouldn't think of going off into the wilderness without lugging a big old tin can along."

"Oh, Ben. You're silly." Liz sat at the table twisting a curl of hair around her finger, watching me dunk pieces of bread into the egg mixture and slap them into the frying pan. "Do you like Lakeview any better now?" she asked.

"Things are starting to look up, I guess."

"Do you have any friends?"

"Sure."

"Why don't you ever bring anybody home with you?"

I flipped the sizzling bread over in the pan. "I'm just too busy working in the shop, that's all. I need to make an appointment to see you lately, though. You're always off with your friends someplace."

Liz looked hurt. "Ben, you're still my best friend."

"Only kidding, Liz. I think it's great that you've made a lot of friends here. I'm proud of you. Here, chow down." I slid a plate of French toast across the table to her, and sat down to eat one myself.

After we finished the food, I headed out for the beach. I hadn't set any particular time with Regina, but I didn't want her to think I wasn't coming.

I climbed up the bank and stood there for a few minutes surveying the beach. From this spot you could see everything but the small section hidden by the point. I didn't see Regina, so I started down the other side of the bank and headed toward the point. From there, I could see all the way down the beach and all the way across the sandbar, but there was no sign of Regina.

Then a voice spoke to me, not more than a few feet from my ear. "Hi, Ben."

"Regina! Where the heck did you come from? Two seconds ago this beach was empty!"

Regina didn't say anything. She just smiled. Well, that made sense. No self-respecting witch was going to let me in on her secrets. I'd just have to get used to her popping in and out like that.

I noticed something else that was strange. Her eyes were a different color today, sort of a pale turquoise. Hey, the lake was the same color! Now that was a really neat trick. I didn't say anything to her about it. I figured I was just supposed to keep quiet about things like that. I didn't want to get on her bad side and have her start zapping me.

I reached in my pocket and pulled out a bag of M&M's. "I brought you a present."

"Oh, thanks, Ben. They're my favorite." We started walking down the beach, away from the sandbar. "I'll show you around, if you want. What would you like to see?"

"How about that lighthouse?" I asked. "I tried to get to it before, but I couldn't make it because of the stream. Is there a way to get out there?"

Regina picked up her pace. "Sure. You'll love it. It feels as if you're on a ship in the middle of the lake. Come on."

She started jogging and I fell into step next to her. After the first five minutes, I was panting for breath and she looked as if she'd been sitting in an armchair, not winded at all. I should have known a witch wouldn't get tired out.

"Hey, I give up," I gasped. "Let's stop for a minute, okay?"

Regina looked surprised, although how she could have missed my wheezing was beyond me. I climbed up on a weedy bank and stretched out.

"I'm sorry, Ben," Regina said, flopping down beside me. "I sort of go into a trance when I jog. It feels really good once you get in practice."

No way! She wasn't putting me into any trances. I'd have to keep on my guard with her. Being friends with a witch was okay if we just did normal stuff, but I wasn't about to get into anything weird. I started to put my arms under my head to make a pillow, when I felt a sudden stinging pain. "Ouch! Something just bit me." We both scrambled to our feet. My elbow was turning red and stinging like crazy. "Must have been a bee down in the grass," I said rubbing the elbow, which made it burn.

"That doesn't look like a bee sting to me," Regina said. She looked around the grass where we'd been lying. "There's your bee," she said, pointing to a tall scraggly plant.

"This thing?" I asked, reaching for it.

Regina grabbed my wrist. "Don't touch it, Ben. That's stinging nettle. Didn't they have it where you came from?"

"If they did, I never ran into it. How does it sting? I don't see any prickers on it."

"The stems have small spines filled with venom. It's very irritating to the skin."

"That's the understatement of the year. Geez! How long will it keep stinging?"

Regina was looking around in the patch of weeds. "Not long, if I can find the antidote for it. It's usually close by. Nature seems to plan it that way. There it is!" She pulled up some long leaves that looked like a huge, twisted dandelion plant.

"What're you going to do with those things?" I asked.

I watched her grind the leaves into the palm of her hand, turning them into a green, squishy blob. "This is curly dock. I'm making a poultice of the leaves. It should take the sting away. Hold it in place with your other hand." She pressed the mess onto my elbow, spreading it out so it covered all of the red area. At first it just felt cold; then I realized the pain was going away.

"That stuff really works. How did you know what to do?"

"My grandmother taught me. She knows about all kinds of healing plants and herbs. Hundreds of years ago that's all they had for medicines and Grandmother says a lot of the ancient cures are just as good as the modern drugs."

"You make it sound as if the whole outdoors is sort of a free drugstore."

Regina smiled. "Well, in a way it is, if you know what to look for."

"So what do you do in winter, when all this stuff is covered with snow?"

"We gather plants all summer and dry them. Then they can be used in the winter to make infusions."

"What's an infusion?"

"You might call it a brew, I guess."

A brew! I knew it. This grandmother must be a witch too. I could picture Regina and her boiling up the potions in a big black cauldron. That thought sort of spooked me, but she sure had cured the sting on my elbow. I could see how having a witch for a friend could be pretty handy, as long as she stayed friendly. Besides, if Regina lived a normal life and went to school and stuff, she was probably only a part-time witch. Maybe just an apprentice.

"Why are you looking at me like that?" Regina asked. "You think I'm odd, don't you?"

"No, Regina, honest."

"Well, I am odd, you know, but that doesn't bother me a bit. I don't want to be like everybody else."

I grinned at her. "Don't worry, you aren't."

Regina punched me in the shoulder, then threw back her head and laughed. I was pretty sure she liked me.

As we started walking along the beach again, she kept pointing out interesting things, like different birds and special kinds of rocks. She seemed to know a lot about the lake and the things around it, but she wasn't trying to show off. You could tell she really loved the place. I'd never met anyone quite like Regina before. She was odd all right, but I liked her anyway.

We went out on a stone jetty and stood looking out across the lake. The size of it still amazed me. "I can't believe how big this thing is. It seems more like an ocean than a lake."

"You think this is big? It's small compared to Lake Huron or Lake Superior. Did you know that half of all the fresh water in the whole world is in the Great Lakes?"

"No kidding?"

"Lake Superior is the deepest of them all, about thirteen hundred feet. Can you imagine? They say the water starts to look dark at two hundred feet and by the time you get to three hundred and fifty feet, it's black as ink."

That was pretty creepy. Leave it to a witch to have that kind of information.

"We studied New York state in Phillipsburg," I said. "But we never had all this lake stuff."

"I learned most of it from my grandmother, not school. She's been telling me stories about the Great Lakes ever since I can remember. She was born on the shore of Lake Huron during the big storm."

"What big storm?"

"It's a long story. I'll tell you about it later. This next part is a little tricky. Follow me."

We had reached the creek. There was a foot-wide section of big jagged rocks exposed along the edges, next to the steep banks on each side. The rocks on our side extended out into the lake as a jetty. On the other side, a pier led out to the lighthouse, forming a channel in between.

Regina moved easily from rock to rock, barely glancing at her feet. I felt my way along, testing out each rock with my foot before I put my weight on it. Every now and then, one of them would tip on its base, nearly dunking me in the water.

Regina called from up ahead. "Come on, Ben. Here's where we get to the other side."

Over her head there was a long, thin tree trunk, spanning the creek from bank to bank about a foot out of reach.

"We're not going to walk over that thing, are we?" My head was spinning just from the thought of it.

"Don't be silly. You just jump up and grab it, then go hand-over-hand until you get to the other side." She sprang up, gripped the trunk and swung out easily for a few steps, then reversed direction and dropped back down next to me. "See? It's easy."

I looked the situation over. It was a good fifteen feet to the other side, and the stream was moving pretty fast. The water was shallow at the edges, where you could see right down to the jagged rocks on the bottom, but it was dark and murky in the center, and I couldn't tell about the depth. "How deep is it out there?"

"I don't know. Over our heads, I guess. I wouldn't want to swim in it, if that's what you mean."

No, that wasn't what I meant, not swimming on purpose, at least. I had some real doubts about making it across that tree trunk. I was probably the worst chin-upper in the history of Phillipsburg Central, and I had never in my life been able to make it all the way across the overhead ladder in the gym. Dropping to the gym floor halfway across the ladder wasn't any picnic, but that would be nothing compared to falling into this.

Regina had already started, and was moving across the tree like a chimpanzee. In fact, I wouldn't have been a bit surprised to see her turn into a chimp right in front of me.

She landed easily on the other bank and turned back to me. "Okay. Come on over, Ben."

My mind was racing, but I couldn't think of any excuse not to do it. I sure wasn't about to let myself be shown up by a girl, even a witch, especially after I pooped out on the jogging. I took a deep breath and jumped for the tree trunk. I got a good, strong grip and started working my way across.

It went pretty well for the first four or five steps. I was a little over a third of the way across, when the muscles in my arms started to get tired. First there was a terrible burning pain from my shoulders to my fingers. I could only move a short distance each time because I wasn't strong enough to hang on with one hand and swing with the other. The next four steps took me to the middle of the log. Suddenly my arm muscles started quivering, and I could feel the bark cutting into my fingers as they began to slip. I looked at the water below me. It was moving much faster than I'd realized, rushing full speed toward the lake.

"Ben, come on. Don't stop now."

I looked over and saw Regina below me on the other bank. She looked a hundred miles away. I wasn't going to make it!

"Ben, don't look down. Keep your eyes on me. *You can do it.*"

She said that very calmly, but with a force I'd never heard from a kid before. She was staring hard with those strange, pale eyes. I felt a sudden tingling on my forehead, right between my eyes.

"Your arms are strong enough to carry you, Ben. Keep coming toward me. Don't look away. *I know you can do it.*"

I felt the tingling move down my neck, out to my shoulders, and down my arms. Of course, that was it! She was putting a spell on me, making me strong. I could feel the energy pouring into my muscles as I took one swing, then another, gaining strength with each one. I felt like Superman! I made it easily to the other side and dropped down beside Regina.

She just smiled at me and turned around as if nothing had happened. "Come on," she said. I could tell you weren't supposed to thank a witch for saving you with a magic spell. It was another one of those things I'd just have to accept and not talk about.

We worked our way down the opposite bank. It was a lot easier than the trip down the other side of the creek had been. Regina seemed to be protecting me from falling in with her magic. When we got back out to the beach, we were at the beginning of the pier. It looked like a raised sidewalk, leading us right out into the lake, the waves gently licking its edges as we walked along.

It wasn't until we reached the end of the pier and looked back that I realized how far out we were. It did feel as if we were on a ship at sea, the lighthouse towering above us like a mast. Regina sat down at its base and pulled out the bag of M&M's.

I found a spot next to her. "Tell me about that big storm," I said.

Regina leaned back against the lighthouse. "All right. It all happened back in November of 1913. My great-grandfather, Hugh La Fleur, was a seaman aboard the ore carrier, *Charles S. Price*. He and his wife, Yvonne, lived right on the southern tip of Lake Huron. There were only three weeks left of the shipping season, before they'd tie up for the winter and the men could head back to their homes. Hugh was anxious to get home to see his wife because she was getting very close to the birth of their first baby. He almost signed off the ship in Cleveland. Then he decided they'd need the extra pay and bonus money for the baby, so he stayed with the ship."

Regina seemed to change as she got into the story, almost as if she were in some kind of trance. She even sounded different — more grown up and mysterious. "It started out like an ordinary winter gale on Saturday, the ninth of November. Many freighters were out on the lakes because they had shipping schedules to finish at the end of the season. The storm hit Lake Huron full force the next day. It was a hurricane, more terrible than any that had ever been seen on the Great Lakes."

She was using her hands now to describe the fury of the storm, and her voice was more urgent. I could almost feel the deck of a ship rocking under me as I listened to her. "The winds reached sixty miles an hour, with gusts up to seventy, and it howled on and on, for sixteen solid hours. The waves were mast-high, thirty-five feet, and came close together, three at a time. They said there were times when the wind was raging in one direction and the sea running in another.

"On shore, it was a terrible blizzard. Yvonne La Fleur was alone and terrified. First of all, she knew her husband's ship was probably out on open water in that storm, and she feared for his life. Then she realized she and her unborn child were in grave danger, too. The winds were tearing at their small farmhouse, which was out in the open itself, on a small bluff just above the coastline. She could hear the angry waves ripping at the beach, and the winds roared down the chimney like a freight train.

"When the storm was at the height of its fury, it suddenly became deathly quiet. That's when Yvonne La Fleur gave birth to her baby — a girl."

"Why was the storm over so fast?" I asked.

"It wasn't over. The calm just meant that the eye of the hurricane was passing over. Then the storm started up again, even harder than before. Yvonne and her baby huddled under a pile of quilts. Yvonne tried to ration the last of the firewood she had stored in the house because she was afraid to go out through the storm to the woodshed. Before it ended, she had broken up most of their furniture to keep the fire going.

"Finally, when the storm was over, Yvonne's father fought through the snow from the town of Port Huron with a horse-drawn sled and rescued them. The spray from the huge waves had covered the entire house with a thick coating of ice, so it took him over an hour to chip away the ice from around the door enough to get it opened. He bundled them up carefully in the sled and took them back into town. Yvonne was terribly worried about her husband, but she clung to the hope that he was still alive. She even refused to name the baby, saying she wanted her husband to choose the name when he came back."

"He couldn't have survived a storm like that, could he?"

"No. Most of the ships out in that storm went down without leaving any survivors. Hugh's body was finally found washed up on the Canadian shore. But something very strange had happened to him."

"What?" I asked, wondering what would seem strange to a witch.

"He was wearing a life belt from the *Regina*, another ship."

"The *Regina*? Is that where your name came from?"

Regina nodded. "When the body of her husband was returned, Yvonne was devastated. She held the life belt in her hands, tracing the faded letters with her finger. No one could explain how the crews of the two ships had come together in the middle of that raging storm. Some people thought that the two freighters had collided and hung together with their decks connected before sinking. There was no mystery in the mind of my great-grandmother, though. She knew her husband had given her a sign. She named the baby Regina."

"Wow," I whispered. "That's quite a story."

"It's all true, every word of it. My grandmother still has that old life belt."

"So the baby was the grandmother you live with now?"

"The same."

"Why were you named after her?" I asked.

Regina took a deep breath and let it out slowly. "I was born on the same date, the tenth of November, so that's why I got her name. But Grandmother and I are alike in other ways too."

"How?" I asked, then wished I had kept my mouth shut. Of course they were alike. They were both witches.

Regina's eyes grew angry. At first I thought she had read my mind. "I lost my father when I was born too, only he wasn't lost at sea. He just got lost, period."

"What do you mean?"

Regina jutted out her chin. "He didn't want to get stuck with a family, so he took off."

"Oh," I mumbled. "That's really tough."

"You think so? That's only half of it. About a year later, after moving around a lot, my mother and I came here to live with Grandmother. One day, my mother said she was going to the store for a carton of milk and never came home. I guess she didn't want a kid either. She left a note that just said, 'I'm sorry.' That was the last we ever heard from her. I was so little at the time, I can't even remember what she looked like."

I didn't know what to say. "That's terrible."

Regina's eyes flashed. "What's terrible? Who wants to be stuck with parents like that? They didn't deserve me anyway. Besides, I love my grandmother. We have a good life together."

"I like your name — Regina — has a nice ring to it."

Regina smiled. "I like it because it gives me roots, connects me to other generations. I think that's important. That's why I love the lakes."

"How can you love the Great Lakes when your great-grandfather was drowned in one of them? Doesn't it make you afraid of the water?"

"The lakes have given my family much more than they've taken away. Most of my ancestors were sailors on the lakes and lived along their shores. I could never move away from here. This is where I belong." She looked out over the lake and her eyes turned exactly the same shade of blue as the water.

8

After hearing the story of the big storm, I had a whole new respect for the lake. I had a new respect for Regina, too, and had pretty much accepted the fact that she was a witch. I liked the way she was proud of her background and wasn't ashamed of the fact that her parents had left her.

Finally, my two-week grounding was over, and Regina and I got to see each other more often. We always met at the beach, on the Lakeview side, not the sandbar. We never went to each other's houses and we never once said anything about her being a witch. It was an unspoken understanding that we had between us. Her magic spells had started making my life a lot better, though, and I never had to come out and ask for help. She seemed to know what I needed without me having to say it.

One day we found an old beat-up soccer ball that somebody had left on the beach. I dribbled it down the beach, then hooked my foot under it to flip it up in the air and did a header.

"You're pretty good at that, Ben. Are you on the soccer team at Westshore?"

"No. I was grounded the week they were having the tryouts for the team. It's too late now. I sure miss it, though. Herbie and I played a lot of soccer in Phillipsburg."

"Maybe it's not too late. Just go to the coach and explain what happened. Ask if you could try out now."

"Me? Explain something to an adult? My tongue turns into a pretzel when I try to talk to anyone over sixteen. I could never pull that off."

"Don't be silly, of course you could. Just go to the coach and talk to him. You can do it, Ben. I know you can."

She was looking at me with those strange eyes — green today — and I suddenly realized what she was doing. I could feel that prickly sensation between my eyes. She was doing her magic on me again, fixing it so I could go talk to the soccer coach.

The feeling was still with me the next morning when I got to school. I got a pass from homeroom and ran down the two flights of stairs to the gym. Coach Bradley was posting the practice schedule for the week on the bulletin board.

"Could I see you for a minute, sir?"

The coach looked up at me. I could tell he didn't remember who I was, even though he had me three times a week in gym. "Yes? What can I do for you?"

I reached out to shake his hand. That surprised him. "My name is Ben Wagner, sir. I know it's late, but I'd like to try out for junior varsity soccer."

"Sorry, kid. Tryouts are over. The team has been working together for some time. I can't put somebody new in now. Maybe next semester."

"If you'd just watch me play, I know I could be a valuable team member."

"So where were you when we had tryouts?"

"I was grounded. I had some trouble at the very beginning of the year, but that's all straightened out."

"Grounded? Who grounded you?"

"My father. I had to work every night in his barbershop for the first two weeks of school. I still work there some nights, but I could work around the soccer schedule."

"Barbershop? Your dad the one who bought Angie Romano's place?"

"Yes, sir."

"I've met him. Nice guy. So you work in the shop some?"

"Yes. Mostly waiting on customers and cleaning up."

"I like to see a kid who does something besides hanging around street corners." He picked up a soccer ball and tossed it to me. "Okay, Wagner, show me what you can do."

I can't even describe what happened next. All I know is I gave one of the most dazzling demonstrations of handling a soccer ball that Coach Bradley had ever seen. Regina's magic was really working. The soccer ball seemed to be connected to me by some strange force. I dribbled the ball up and down the gym floor, dodging imaginary opponents as I went, and it seemed to hover right in front of my foot. I even surprised myself. I'd always been a better than average soccer player, but nothing like this!

Coach Bradley finally blew his whistle. "Okay, okay! I've seen enough. I don't usually bend the rules, but I'd be a fool to keep a player like you off the team. Come to practice tonight, right after school."

"Thank you, sir. You won't regret it, I promise."

I was all set for practice. I'd already put my shin guards in my backpack, just in case.

*

I couldn't wait to tell Regina about making the team. I found her sitting out on the jetty.

"I made it, Regina. You should've seen me. I zoomed around the gym like Pelé. It was wonderful. Coach Bradley just stood there with his eyes bugging out of his head."

"That's great, Ben. I knew you could do it."

"You don't even seem surprised. You don't understand what a big deal this is." That was the only trouble with having a girl for a friend. Herbie would've been doing handstands over this, but Regina just sat there smiling.

"I know making the soccer team is important to you,

Ben, and I'm excited for you. I'm just not surprised, that's all." Sure. Why would she be surprised? She'd made it happen.

"Now if I can just keep my grades up, so I can stay on the team."

"Are you having trouble in classes?"

"Well, science and social studies are okay, but I've always had a hard time with English and math. The teachers go so fast when they're explaining things, I just don't get it."

"Why don't you go up to them after school and ask them to help you with the things you don't understand?"

"Regina, you know I can't talk to . . ."

"Oh, I forgot. Old pretzel-tongue, right? I thought we took care of that back when you went to see the soccer coach. If you could convince him to take you on the team, you certainly shouldn't have any trouble asking a couple of teachers for help. I know you can do it, Ben."

She had that special look in her eyes again. "Oh . . . yeah," I mumbled, as the light began to dawn. Sure enough, if I thought about it, I could start to feel that tingle in my forehead again. "I see what you're saying. You mean I can *do* it."

"Yes, that's what I said. You can be really weird sometimes, Ben."

Me, weird? A witch was calling *me* weird? Well, I figured she could call me anything she wanted to, if she'd keep her magic spells coming.

*

Life was getting to be just about perfect, after Regina sent me to talk to my math and English teachers. I didn't have any trouble explaining my problems to them, not even old Mr. Hyman, the math teacher. I still wasn't the best student in the world, but I was giving it my best shot, and from then on I wasn't afraid to ask for help when I didn't understand something. Susan was still spying on me in school, but things were going so well for me, she wasn't getting any more ammunition for blackmail.

The only thing that really bothered me was not being able to talk with Dad. I could speak up with everybody else — why not him? I wanted to bring up the subject with Regina, but I had the feeling her magic couldn't help me with that problem. There were some things even a witch couldn't do anything about.

The days were getting pretty short now. I usually had soccer practice or games after school, so Regina and I always had a million things to tell each other by the time the weekend rolled around.

Liz stopped me one Sunday afternoon as I was getting ready to head out for the beach to meet Regina. She didn't look as chipper as usual.

"Ben, can you do me a favor?"

"Sure, Liz, what's up?"

"Could you . . . would you give me . . . oh, never mind." Liz was looking down at her feet as she talked, wrapping one foot around the leg of the kitchen table.

"Hurry up, squirt. Out with it. I have to get going."

Liz started to leave the kitchen. "Never mind, Ben. It was nothing."

"You sure?" I asked.

She ran up the stairs without answering. I sat there for a minute, debating whether or not to go upstairs and question her some more. Then I decided it could wait until later, because I wanted to get to the beach. A small nagging doubt kept brushing the edges of my mind as I walked toward the lake, but as soon as I saw Regina running toward me, all thoughts of Liz were forgotten.

"The water's pretty rough today," Regina shouted over the crashing of the waves. "It's exciting to go out to the lighthouse when it's like this. Want to try it?"

This was the first time I'd seen the lake when it was really riled up. There were whitecaps all the way to the horizon line. "Yeah, I guess I'm game, if you are."

We'd made the trip over the log bridge so many times now, it didn't bother me at all. It was hard to believe I'd almost fallen in the first time. We stopped when we got to the pier. Waves were breaking over the edge of the concrete here and there.

"You have to be careful on the way out, Ben. Watch how the waves are coming in so you can move between them as they come up over the sides."

"I don't mind getting my feet wet."

"No, it's more than that. Every now and then there's a really powerful wave that can pull at you and throw you off balance. Besides, the pier gets slippery when it's wet."

By the time we reached the end of the pier, the waves

were breaking hard against the cement platform. We climbed up the steps to the lighthouse entrance to get beyond the reach of the spray.

"Boy, this is really something," I said. "If it's this bad in the fall, I can imagine how scary the winter storms must be. No wonder they lost so many ships back in the big storm. Does Lake Ontario ever freeze over, all the way to Canada?"

"Very rarely. I remember it happening just once. Most winters the water never gets below forty degrees. That's why the lake has such an effect on our winter weather."

"How?"

"Well, it holds its warmth in the fall, and cools off much more slowly than the air. The warm air rises off the lake, carrying a lot of moisture, and when it moves out over the land, it dumps the moisture as snow. The areas just south and east of the lakes are hit the hardest. It's called lake effect snow."

"We used to get tons of snow in Phillipsburg, and we weren't anywhere near a lake."

"You were close enough to Lake Erie to get lake effect storms from it. The higher the winds, the farther the storms can travel, sometimes over a hundred miles. Lake effect storms from Lake Erie can get almost to Rochester if the winds are right. We've had some pretty wicked winters around here."

"How many years have you lived here, out on the sandbar?" I asked.

The waves were breaking harder against the lighthouse platform now, and Regina pulled up the hood of her nylon shell to shield herself from the spray. "Since I was a baby. My grandmother has lived here for years. Our cottage was built by one of my ancestors over a hundred years ago. Since then there's always been a member of our family living in it."

I thought about what Mr. Romano had said about a family of witches living on the sandbar for generations. Boy, would he be surprised if he knew one of them was my best friend. "What's your grandmother like?"

"She's . . . well, she's different, but nice. I guess she isn't like most grandmothers. She's taught me a lot, though."

"Do you and your grandmother talk much?"

"What kind of a question is that? We live together. Of course we talk."

"I don't mean just talk. I mean . . . you know . . . talk."

Regina rolled her eyes. "Honestly, Ben. Do you mean can I talk to her about things that are important to me? Like feelings?"

"Yeah," I said, relieved that she'd figured it out. "Can you?"

"Sure. Grandmother and I are very close. She's all the family I ever had. Why? Can't you do that with your parents?"

"Well, Mom listens to me sometimes, I guess, but not Dad. I can never make him see my side of things."

"Have you really tried to get through to him?"

"Sure. Lots of times. But it's no use."

"If I had a father, I'd do everything I could to break

down that wall. You don't know how lucky you are to have a whole family, Ben."

I was just about to hint around about a magic spell to help me talk to my dad, when Regina was distracted by some black clouds tumbling across the sky.

"What's the matter?" I asked.

"The wind is picking up fast. I didn't notice the storm coming on. I think we'd better get back in while we still can."

"You really think it's going to get that bad?"

"Things can change fast on this lake. Look over there, at the Coast Guard station. They're putting up a storm warning."

I could see a flag whipping in the wind as it was hoisted up the flagpole. "Does each flag mean something different?" I asked.

"Yes. One red triangle is a small craft advisory. That's what was up first thing this morning. The one that's going up now, the red rectangle with a black rectangle in the center, is a storm warning. I should have been paying more attention. Come on. Let's go back."

The waves were clawing at the pier from both sides now, with barely any space between them. Regina clutched my arm. "If we hang on to each other and move along carefully, we'll be all right. Just brace yourself for the waves."

"Okay, let's go. We'll make it," I said, with a confidence I didn't feel. Regina seemed scared, which bothered me because that must mean her magic powers didn't have any effect on the lake.

Soon after we started out, a wave hit us from the left and shot high in the air, crashing down over our heads. It pushed our upper bodies to the right, then immediately pulled our feet to the left, as it slid back into the water. My feet started to go out from under me, but Regina held firm. "Stop, Ben," she shouted in my ear. "Don't try to move ahead when a wave hits. Just plant both feet and hold on."

After a few more waves, I knew what to expect, and we were making some progress, but the beach still looked far away. I'd been too scared to notice how cold it was when we first got soaked, but now the water felt like ice. We were bracing ourselves, waiting for the next big wave to pass, when Regina noticed something on shore.

"Ben, look at that little girl out on the end of the jetty. If she climbs down any farther she's liable to get washed off those rocks."

"Where?" I asked, just as a wave split over our heads, wiping out my view.

"I can't see her now," Regina said, as the spray cleared. "No, wait, there she is, right down by the water. She seems to be hiding from someone. She just ducked down behind that big square boulder. There! See her red hair?"

"Red hair?" The child peeked up over the rock and I saw her. It was Liz! "Regina! That's my sister! What's she doing here?"

"We have to get her out of there, Ben!"

Regina and I started running back down the pier, not even waiting for the waves to pass. I saw Liz stand up and start to climb back up on the jetty, just as a huge

90

wave broke right over her. When the wave subsided, Liz wasn't there anymore.

"She's gone! Liz is gone!" I shouted.

"There she is Ben, in the water, about ten feet out."

We kept running and I was taken by surprise by another wave, which sent me sprawling. I felt my chin grind into the hard cement, but my only thought was to get back on my feet and reach Liz. I saw Liz's head bobbing up above the surface, then she started to slip under. We were almost opposite her now, about thirty feet away.

"I'm going in after her," I said, pulling off my sneakers.

"I'll run for help!"

I saw Liz's head come up again, and I dove out as far as I could. I lost sight of her as soon as I hit the water because of the waves. My arms were churning like a windmill, but I didn't seem to be getting anywhere. Each time I got caught in a trough between two waves, it was like swimming uphill. I went up over one swell after another, but couldn't see any sign of her.

Suddenly, my hand struck something soft. I grabbed as hard as I could and realized I had the back of Liz's jacket. I pulled up with all my strength and adjusted my hold so I could get her head up out of the water. Liz was thrashing, fighting me. We both went under, and I didn't have a chance to get any air. I felt as if my lungs were going to split open as we went down, and bubbles were pouring out of Liz's mouth. I kicked hard and pulled with my free arm. Somehow we managed to explode through the surface again. Liz was quiet now, not fighting me anymore. I refused to let my mind think about what that might mean.

It had been hard enough to make any progress when I was swimming alone, but now it was impossible. Each wave washed away a little more of my strength. I'd been right. Regina's magic was useless against the power of the lake.

A wave swelled up under us, lifting us to where I could see the beach. We'd been pulled over to the east of the jetty. I'd been swimming in the wrong direction, sideways, instead of toward shore. Regina was on the beach, shouting to me. Her voice barely carried out to me over the sound of the wind.

"Come on, Ben! You can do it!"

As soon as I heard her voice, I felt the strength starting to pour back into me. I shifted Liz to my left arm, so I could swim with my right, and headed for shore. Regina's words chanted in my mind with the rhythm of each stroke.

"You can do it! . . . You can do it! . . . You can do it!"

The magic was working! Regina might not have any power over the lake, but she'd given me the power to fight it. I don't know how long I kept swimming like that. I didn't think about time, but just concentrated on pulling us ahead, one stroke after another. We were lifted up over another swell and I could see other people running down the beach. I closed my eyes and kept pulling with every bit of strength I had. Suddenly, there were voices . . . and hands grabbing us . . . lifting us out of the water. Regina had called the rescue squad.

"Get the girl first."

"She's not breathing."

"I'm not getting a pulse here."

Two medics were crouched over Liz's limp form on the beach. One of the medics tilted Liz's head back, held her mouth open, and pinched her nose with his other hand.

"Okay! Her airway's clear."

He breathed into Liz's mouth, then the other medic pushed on her chest, counting out loud.

"One one-thousand, two one-thousand, three one-thousand, four one-thousand, five one-thousand."

They were taking turns, one breathing into her mouth, the other pushing on her chest. I knew they were doing CPR. The Phillipsburg Fire Department had come to school one day to show us how to do it. Another medic came up to me and put a blanket around my shoulders. "What's your name, son?"

"Ben Wagner."

"How are you feeling, Ben? Do you hurt anywhere, or feel sick to your stomach?"

I tried to see around him, to watch what was happening with Liz. Two other men were sliding some kind of board under her without interrupting the CPR.

"I'm okay," I said, coughing. "Just take care of my sister."

The medic moved into my line of vision. "They're taking care of her. I want to check you out. Let's get a quick listen to your lungs and make sure you're not carrying any of the lake around with you." He had pulled my shirt up and was moving a stethoscope around on my back and chest. "Sounds good, Ben. That looks like a nasty scrape on your chin. How did you get it? Do you remember?"

The four men were lifting Liz now, moving up the bank with her, never missing a beat of the CPR. I scrambled to my feet. "I just bumped it. It's okay." The medic grabbed my arm and we followed the others up the slope.

"Take it easy, Ben," he said. "You've been through a lot. That was some rescue you just pulled off."

We were beside the waiting ambulance now. While they were sliding the stretcher into the back of the ambulance, the driver punched some buttons on the radio.

"This is Lakeview ambulance, sixteen-fourteen."

There was some static, then a voice came back. "This is Rochester General. Go ahead, Lakeview."

"We're coming in with a five hundred. The patient is a drowning victim, female, approximately seven years old. No pulse. No respiration. We're administering CPR. Our ETA at Rochester General is four minutes."

The crackling again. "Ten-four, Lakeview. You are clear to come in to our facility."

The back doors of the ambulance slammed with a deep thud. A policeman motioned back the crowd that had pushed close around us. The flashing red light turned everything blood-red, and the siren started screaming as the ambulance pulled away.

A tall kid squeezed through the crowd next to me. "What happened?" he asked.

The man in front of us turned around. "A little kid drowned," he said.

"No, she didn't!" I yelled. "She's not dead! She's my sister!"

I could feel the crowd around me start to pull back. A policeman put his arm around my shoulder and Regina slipped in on the other side of me, taking my hand. "She'll be all right," she whispered. "You saved her."

"Take it easy, son," the policeman said, as he patted my shoulder. "Your sister's in good hands, thanks to you. Let's go find your parents."

I stood frozen for a minute, watching the flashing light of the ambulance as it sped away. Liz just had to pull through. With each flash of the revolving red light, the voice in my mind chanted, "You can do it! . . . You can do it! . . . You can do it."

9

The policeman put me in his car and his partner questioned me about what had happened as we drove over to the barbershop to pick up Dad. I don't think I was able to give him many answers. Things were all blurring together in my head. Dad was sweeping up as we walked in.

"Mr. Wagner?"

Dad looked up, smiling, but his expression changed when he saw us.

"Yes? Ben! What happened?"

I couldn't even talk. Water was dripping from my hair, partly hiding the fact that I was crying.

"There's been an accident at the beach, sir," the policeman continued. "Your daughter . . ."

"Susan? What's happened to Susan?" Dad set aside his broom and Mr. Romano came over, putting a hand on Dad's shoulder.

"It's Liz, Dad," I sobbed.

"Liz? At the beach? Where is she now?" Dad asked, looking back and forth between the policeman's face and mine.

"She's being taken to Rochester General, Mr. Wagner. I'll take you over there. Do you want to stop and get your wife?"

"I saw the ambulance go by. I never dreamed. . . . Yes. Yes, of course. Let's go."

Mr. Romano put his arm around me. "What about Ben? Are you taking him to the hospital?"

The policeman shook his head. "It's not necessary. He was checked out by a medic. What he really needs right now is to get out of those wet clothes and get warmed up."

"I'll take care of that," Mr. Romano said.

"Thanks, Angie." Dad pulled off his white barber coat and grabbed his jacket. He turned to the policeman. "Let's get going."

There were more sirens as the police car headed out. Suddenly I started to shake so hard my teeth were actually banging together. I couldn't do anything to stop it.

"It's okay, Ben," Mr. Romano said, rubbing my hair with a clean towel. "Take it easy, now. Let's go upstairs. I'm sure my wife can find some dry clothes to fit you."

As we started up the stairs at the back of the shop to the Romanos' apartment, we were almost run down by Mrs. Romano, who was on her way down.

"Angie, the sirens! The police! What's going on?"

"Come back upstairs, Anna. We have to get Ben warmed up."

Mrs. Romano took one look at me and didn't ask any more questions. She went in to run a tub of hot water.

"Get those clothes off, Ben, and get in the tub. You're freezing. When you come out, I'll give you some hot soup." She left a big bath towel for me and a soft, warm-looking bathrobe. I closed the bathroom door, glad to be alone, and stripped off my wet clothes. I slid down into the steaming water, but the shaking didn't stop for a long time.

All I could think of was poor Liz. Why hadn't I listened to her this morning? I'd been so anxious to get out of the house, I didn't bother to find out what was wrong. Whatever she wanted must have been really important for her to follow me out to the lighthouse like that, and I let her down. If anything happened to her, I'd be the one to blame. I slid down in the tub and let my tears run right into the water.

In a little while, there was a knock on the bathroom door. "Ben, Anna's got some soup made. Ben? You all right?"

"Yes, Mr. Romano. I'll be right out." I dried off and put on the bathrobe. I was warm enough now, but I still had a shivery feeling inside, the kind of shiver that had nothing to do with being cold.

The soup was homemade, a golden chicken soup with little meatballs in it, but I could barely make my throat open up enough to swallow it. Mrs. Romano sat at the kitchen table with me, trying to encourage me to eat.

"It tastes really good, Mrs. Romano," I said, not wanting to hurt her feelings, "but I guess I'm not very hungry."

"Just try some more, Ben. You need to warm up your insides."

I was saved by the bell. Mrs. Romano ran to answer the telephone.

"Yes, George. How is she?" There was a long silence on our end while Mrs. Romano just listened, shaking her head and clicking her tongue.

"I'm sure she'll be all right, George. We'll be praying for her." There was another pause. "Really? No, I didn't know. He hasn't said anything. Here, I'll put him on." She handed me the receiver, smiling.

My father's voice sounded far away. "Ben, are you all right? I ran out so fast, I never asked you."

"Yes, sir, I'm fine. How's Liz?"

"We don't know yet. She's breathing on her own now, but it's too soon to tell. They still have her in the emergency room." Dad cleared his throat. "Ben, the police told me what you did, how you pulled her out of the water. Liz owes her life to you. We're all very grateful, son."

When they found out it was my fault in the first place, Mom and Dad would hate me, especially if Liz didn't pull through. I couldn't think of anything to say to him.

I just handed the phone back to Mrs. Romano and left the room.

I could hear her talking in the distance. "He's been through a lot, George, but I think he's all right. It's best that he doesn't go to the hospital tonight. I'm going to get him settled in bed."

Mrs. Romano led me to a spare bedroom. "I just made this bed up fresh for you. Sleep is the best thing for you now, Ben. I'm going to church, to light candles for your sister."

I wished there was something I could do for Liz, but I couldn't think of a thing. I tried a few prayers, but I had as much trouble talking to God as I did trying to talk to my Dad. I just lay on the bed, listening to people come and go, and watching the lights of passing cars reflect across the ceiling.

*

I was having breakfast the next morning with Mrs. Romano and two of her teenage sons, Carlo and Tony. Everybody seemed to be talking at once. I was doing my best to shove down some scrambled eggs, but I still had that big lump in my throat, like I was going to cry any minute. Mr. Romano burst in with the morning paper. "Ben, look! You're famous!"

He held up the local section of the *Times-Chronicle*, and there I was, a huge picture of me huddled in a blanket, staring off into space with a look of horror in my eyes. Across the top of the page was the headline, LAKEVIEW BOY RESCUES SISTER FROM LAKE.

"Listen to this," Mr. Romano said, putting on his glasses to read the small print.

> At the height of yesterday afternoon's storm, Benjamin Wagner of Lakeview showed courage far beyond his twelve years when his sister, Elizabeth, seven, was swept into the turbulent waters off Lakeview Beach. Wagner and his companion, Regina St. Clair, also of Lakeview, were on the Lakeview pier when the incident occurred. Wagner dove into the lake and swam through four-foot waves to reach his sister. St. Clair ran to a nearby house to summon the Lakeview Rescue Squad, which arrived just as Wagner and his sister were reaching the shoreline.
> Daniel D'Amato, Rescue Squad Coordinator, was one of the first on the scene. According to D'Amato, the task was almost impossible for a boy Wagner's age and size. "A lot of grown men would have been turned back by those waves," D'Amato said. "That boy deserves a medal for what he did."
> Elizabeth and Benjamin are the children of Mr. and Mrs. George Wagner of Summerville Drive in Lakeview. Elizabeth Wagner is currently listed in critical condition at Rochester General Hospital.

This was terrible. Everybody thought I was a big hero now, and only I knew the truth, just me and Liz, but she might never. . . .

"So we have a real hero in our house!" Carlo was pounding me on the back. "That's terrific, Ben. You must be really proud."

Tony was examining a map that was next to my picture. "Look, Ben. This shows how far you swam to get your sister. You must be some swimmer." There was a diagram of the pier, with an X where Liz fell in and a dotted line that showed my path in the water. It all seemed as if it had happened to somebody else, not me. Why not? I had been somebody else at the time. I'd been under the spell of a witch.

"Yeah, well . . . I've got to get going. I'll miss the school bus. Thanks for everything," I said, and bounded down the stairs before anybody could answer. I just wanted to get away, so I didn't have to talk about it.

I hadn't planned on the reception I got in school. People I didn't even know came up to talk to me. It seemed as if the whole world had heard about the accident by now. We had an assembly third period, and I sat in a back corner, trying not to be noticed.

Mr. Ramsey got up to make announcements. "As most of you probably have heard, one of our students made the newspaper headlines this morning." Oh, no! There was a rustling in the auditorium, and people were craning around in their seats to see me.

Mr. Ramsey went on and on. I didn't even listen to what he was saying. I felt trapped. "Now let's all give a big hand to our own Westshore High hero, Ben Wagner." The whole auditorium exploded with applause, and everybody jumped up to their feet. They had all turned around, looking at me, smiling, clapping, whistling. I wanted to scream out that I didn't deserve it, but I just sat there, waiting for it all to end.

Finally it was over, and the lights went down for a preview scene from the fall musical. I slipped out of my seat and left the auditorium to the sound of tap dancing.

I had to get to Mom and Dad, to tell them the truth before this thing got any more out of hand.

I'd seen the hospital before, when we'd gone by in the car, and knew if I just kept walking down Ridge Road, I'd come to it in four or five miles. I thought about taking a bus, but decided I needed the time to think.

It bothered me that people were giving me so much attention for something I didn't even do. After all, it was Regina's magic that saved Liz, not me. The guy in the paper had even said it was impossible for a kid my age to have done what I did. That proved it.

I was passing a lot of stores and a couple of smaller shopping centers. There was a ton of traffic. I had no idea there were so many people out driving around while we were in school. I could see the hospital in the distance. I was sure Dad and Mom would be there. I realized I hadn't seen Susan on the bus this morning. I wondered if she was staying with some of those rich friends of hers. The thought of living in a family with Susan as my only sister suddenly hit me. There was no way I'd stay around if Liz didn't pull through. I'd run away from home. I'd just have to make the best of it. If Regina had managed most of her life without any parents, so could I. I wondered if Regina had seen the newspaper.

If only we'd never left Phillipsburg. I wanted everything to go back the way it was, just hanging around with Herbie at the crick. Maybe I'd run away to Phillipsburg and live with Herbie's family. It would be good to be back in familiar territory again. I knew I'd miss Regina, though. She was my best friend now.

A little red-headed girl and her mother passed me on the sidewalk. For a second I thought it was Liz and my heart practically jumped into my throat. I couldn't believe I might never see her again.

I'd been so lost in my thoughts, I hadn't realized how far I'd walked. When I looked up, I only had to cross a bridge over the expressway and I'd be at the hospital. For a few seconds, I almost chickened out, but I knew I had to find out about Liz. I ran all the rest of the way in.

There was a big curved information desk in the main lobby.

"Are you here with someone?" The blue-haired lady behind the desk looked as if she didn't approve of kids visiting in the hospital.

"I'm supposed to meet my parents. My sister was brought in to emergency yesterday."

"Your sister's name?"

"Elizabeth Wagner."

She flipped through a rotary file, tipping her nose up in the air so she could see through the bottom part of her glasses. "She's in room 520. Follow the blue line to the first bank of elevators. Go up to the fifth floor and turn left."

I got off the elevator on the fifth floor and started looking for room numbers, until I heard someone call my name. I looked up and saw Mom coming down the hall. She looked terrible.

"Oh, Ben," she said, hugging me. But then she couldn't say anything else because she was crying. Dad came up behind her.

"What's happened?" I asked, not wanting to hear the answer.

"Your mom is just exhausted, Ben. We haven't slept at all. Liz is doing pretty well now, though. She has a type of pneumonia, from the water getting into her lungs, but she's over the worst time. She's even been talking a little this morning. She keeps asking for you."

"Is it okay for me to go in?" I asked.

"We have to wait a few minutes," Mom said, wiping her eyes. "The doctor is in with her now. Come to the waiting room with us. Susan's there. Your father went back home to get her after the accident, so she spent the night here, too."

Susan was half asleep on one of the orange couches in the waiting room. She looked up when we went in, but didn't say anything. I could tell she'd been crying. Maybe old Susan had a heart after all.

Dad put his arm around my shoulder. The only other time I could remember him doing that was a couple of years ago when our old golden retriever, Sandy, got run over.

"I called Angie this morning to see how you were doing. He said you went to school."

"Yeah, I did, but I wanted to come over here. I guess I'm cutting class. I didn't tell anybody. I just left."

Dad rubbed my back. "Don't worry about it, son. You should be here with us. I'll go call the school now and tell them you're here, in case they're worried about you."

I felt even worse, now that Dad and Mom were being so nice to me. That wouldn't last for long. I'd have to tell them the truth as soon as Dad got back. Wait till they heard that Liz had asked for my help and I was too busy to listen.

Just then, the doctor came out of Liz's room and walked over to us.

"She's doing very well, Mrs. Wagner, considering what she's been through. I think we can discontinue the oxygen by tonight. If all goes well, we should be discharging her in two or three days." He looked over at me. "You must be Ben. I recognize you from the picture in the paper."

"Yes, sir."

He shook my hand, using both of his hands. "You're a remarkable boy, Ben. That little redhead in there owes her life to you. Why don't you go in? She keeps asking to see you."

"Yes, sir."

I went over to Liz's room and pushed open the door very slowly. Liz looked so tiny in the big hospital bed. Her eyes were closed, and she had a tube going into one arm and another in her nose. How could I have done this to her? I just stood by her bed for a few minutes, watching her. Gradually, her eyelids fluttered, then opened.

"Ben? Oh, Ben, I'm so sorry." She reached for me with the arm that didn't have a tube in it, and started to cry.

"Shh. Take it easy, Liz," I said, taking her hand. "You don't need to be sorry about anything. It was all my fault, for running off and not helping you when you needed me. If I'd taken the time to listen to you at home, you wouldn't have followed me to the lake."

"No, Ben. It wasn't like that at all."

Just then, Mom and Dad came in. Susan was right behind them, peering over Mom's shoulder with a funny expression on her face.

Mom had put on some makeup, but it didn't hide the circles under her eyes. She tried to manage a bright smile. "Isn't it nice to see Ben, honey? Susan is here, too."

Liz's eyes grew wide. "No, not Susan! I don't want Susan in here! Get her out!"

Susan backed out of the room, looking as if she'd been slapped in the face.

Mom put her hand on Liz's forehead. "Calm down, honey. You're not supposed to get excited. Just be quiet now."

"No. I have to tell you about it, all of it. I don't care if Susan does tell you about the vase. It doesn't matter anymore. I won't let her scare me ever again."

Mom whispered to Dad, "Maybe her fever is up again. She's not making any sense. I'll go ask the nurse if she needs some medication. She shouldn't get upset like this."

"Wait, Mom," I said. "I think Liz knows what she's talking about. What about Susan, Liz?"

"Susan made me go to the lake."

Dad turned to me. "Didn't Liz go with you, Ben?"

Liz spoke up before I could answer. "No, Daddy. Ben didn't even know I was there. Susan was mad because I couldn't ask Ben to give me money, so she told me to follow him and spy on him. She wanted to catch him doing something bad so she could blackmail him and get the money that way." Liz looked at me. "I didn't want to spy on you, Ben. Susan said she'd tell on me for breaking Grandma's vase if I didn't."

Mom came over to Liz. "You broke the vase? But I thought the movers . . ."

"Susan made me help her unpack, but when I lifted the vase it was too heavy and I let it drop. Then she said to put all the pieces back in the box so you wouldn't know I did it. That's why I needed to get money for her . . . so she wouldn't tell."

"This doesn't make any sense," Mom said. "Susan has plenty of money from her allowance and babysitting. She must have been teasing you, Liz."

Liz tried to shake her head, but couldn't because of the tube in her nose. "Susan wasn't teasing, Mommy. She meant it. She needs lots of money now, because she wants fancy clothes so she can look like all those snooty rich friends of hers. Susan is the one who's been taking money from your grocery jar. I saw her do it, but I knew you wouldn't believe me, so I never told on her."

Dad turned to me. "Ben? Did you have any idea this was going on?"

"No, sir. I know Liz is telling the truth, though. Susan used to do the same kind of thing to me."

Dad's face was starting to get red. "Liz, let me get this straight. Are you telling me that your sister sent you out alone to follow Ben to the lake?"

"Yes, Daddy."

"I think we all have a lot of talking to do," he said.

"But not here. Let's get home and give Liz a chance to rest."

"But Daddy. . . ." Liz's eyes started to fill up with tears. "Please listen. You never pay any attention to what Ben and I say."

Dad leaned over to kiss her on the forehead. "Don't worry, pumpkin. I'm going to get to the bottom of this. You calm down and get some sleep."

Mom and Dad went on ahead and I was just starting to follow them when Liz grabbed my hand. "Do you think Susan will still bother us after this?" she whispered.

I grinned at her. "No, Liz. I think you just put old Susan out of business."

10

Susan knew she was in for it. She didn't say a word on the way home and she ran up to her room as soon as we got there. We barely made it into the house before the neighbors started coming over, asking about Liz and leaving casseroles and cakes. I didn't realize so many people in the neighborhood even knew us yet. The lady from next door left a platter of ham sandwiches and a big, steaming pot of soup. Mom went upstairs to talk to Susan, leaving Dad and me alone.

Dad ladled out a bowl of soup for each of us, and we dove into the sandwiches. I was practically starving. We just ate for a while without saying anything. Dad looked worried, and every now and then he shook his head, as if he were talking to himself. Then he started looking at me, just staring. I concentrated on my soup and pretended I didn't notice, but he was making me feel uncomfortable.

"Ben, I want to understand what's been happening here, before I talk to Susan. Can you answer a few questions?"

"Yes, sir."

"You said Susan's been doing the same thing to you as she just did to Liz?"

"Yes, sir."

"What kinds of things would she do?"

"Little stuff, mostly. She was just always there when I did something wrong. Then she'd make up a lie so I wouldn't get in trouble and I'd have to give her something later so she wouldn't tell on me."

Dad leaned forward on the table. "Like what? Give me an example."

"Well, one time a couple of years ago I was mowing the lawn with the tractor and I accidentally ran over half a row of beans on the edge of the garden. Susan told me I'd be grounded for a month if you found out, so she told me to clear away the mowed-off tops of the plants. Then she went and told you she'd seen a woodchuck in the garden. You believed her, so to pay her back I had to give her my allowance for a whole month."

Dad rubbed his chin. "I remember that. I sat out by the garden with my shotgun every night for a week waiting to nail that woodchuck. I wondered why he never came back. So Susan would cover up for you, then threaten to tell on you if you didn't give her money."

"Yeah, sort of, only it wasn't always money. When we

111

were younger, it was candy. She always got some of my candy at Halloween and Easter. She even made me give her my big chocolate rabbit the year I broke the window in the barn."

"Did you have any idea she was doing the same thing to Liz?"

"No, but I should have figured that she would . . . especially since she hasn't been able to blackmail me for anything lately."

"Come on, Ben. Blackmail? Aren't you exaggerating things just a bit here?" Dad just sat there staring into his soup for a couple of minutes. Then he shook his head and looked up at me. "I can't imagine Susan doing these things. Your mother and I would have seen all this going on. We're not blind."

So . . . after all that had happened, he still wasn't going to believe me. If he doubted me now, before he even talked to Susan, I didn't stand a chance. She was probably rehearsing her story right now in front of the mirror in her room. She'd memorize a list of all the bad things I'd ever done to spout off to Dad. I couldn't win in this family. The rest of the world thought I was a big-deal hero, but my own father didn't believe a word I said.

"Ben, can you explain why you just sat back and took that kind of treatment from Susan all those years?"

I couldn't think of anything to say. I felt a rage building up inside of me.

"Well?" Dad was raising his voice again.

"No, sir." The words practically caught in my throat.

Dad slammed his fist down on the table. "Damn it, Ben! We almost lost Liz because of this stupid game you kids have been playing. Don't just sit there like a dummy. Speak up! Why do I always feel there's a wall between us?"

"Because there is a wall," I shouted. "You always believe Susan and never listen to me. She's just a good actress, Dad. You and Mom think she's perfect. Why did you even bother having Liz and me? You would've been happier if we'd never been born!"

Dad got up from his chair and started coming around the table. He had an expression on his face that I'd never seen before, all twisted up, like he was about to explode. He grabbed my arm and pulled me up out of my seat. I ducked my head but he didn't hit me. He hugged me — hard.

"Ben . . . Ben . . . how did we get this far off the track, you and me?" I could feel his breath blowing the hair on the top of my head as he talked. "Of course we love you and Liz, every bit as much as we love Susan. Don't you know how proud we are of you?"

"If you mean about me rescuing Liz, Dad, I didn't really. . ."

"I'm not just talking about the rescue, Ben. I'm proud of you for working hard and trying to make the best of this move, even though I know you wanted to stay in Phillipsburg. You had that problem in school at first, but then you straightened out."

"That's another thing," I yelled, pushing away from him. "Susan can twist things around so everything's

113

backwards. I tried to tell you what happened the first day of school, but she got to you first with her lies, and you believed her instead."

I didn't realize that Mom had come into the room. "I think we need to hear what Ben is saying, George. Things have been going on in this family that we haven't been seeing."

"I tried to tell you, too, Mom, about the first day of school. Remember? You didn't listen to me either."

Dad just looked at me for a minute, then pulled out a chair and sat down. "We're listening now, son," he said quietly. "Let's hear about that first day of school . . . from the beginning."

I told them the whole thing, about not finding my homeroom, and being picked up by the sweep, and how Susan tried to blackmail me at lunch. They just sat there listening, never interrupting, just listening, and for the very first time in my life, I really talked to my parents.

When I had finished, Dad stood up. "All right, Ben. I believe you. Now let's get Susan down here and hear her side of it." He went to the bottom of the stairs and called her. It took a few minutes before she came down. When she did, her eyes were all red from crying, but I could tell she was going to try to pull something.

"Sit down, Susan," Dad said. "We have to get a few things straightened out here. You remember the first day of school, when Ben got into all that trouble?"

"Yes, Daddy."

"The story Ben told us about that day doesn't match up with yours. You want another chance to describe it?"

114

"It was just the way I told you before, Daddy. It wasn't Ben's fault. The kids were teasing him and they dared him. . ."

"That's not true, Susan," I yelled.

Dad held up his hand. "Quiet, Ben. You've had your turn. Okay, Susan. I want you to think twice before you go on."

Susan started picking at her fingernails and I noticed they weren't long anymore. They were all chewed down like mine.

"You want to tell us now, Susan?" Dad asked.

"All right. I made it up," she said. "Is that what you want to hear?"

"Only if it's the truth," Dad said.

Susan's lower lip was trembling. "It is."

"What about sending Liz out to the lake?" Mom asked. "I can't believe you'd be foolish enough to do a thing like that."

Susan gripped the edge of the table. "Don't you think I feel terrible about that? I didn't realize the lake was so dangerous. And I never dreamed she'd end up in the water."

"What did Liz mean about you needing money to impress your rich friends?" Mom asked. "What kind of friends are they if they won't accept you the way you are?"

Susan started to cry. I'd never seen her do that before, except when she was trying to get something out of Mom and Dad. This time I was pretty sure it was for real. "They aren't my friends, Mother. I never really fit in

115

with them, no matter how hard I tried. Now they won't have anything to do with me at all. With all the publicity about Liz, they know where I live and everything."

"You mean you were even lying about that?" I asked.

She wiped her eyes. "Well, I didn't mean to, but that first day on the bus, one of the girls asked me if we had moved into one of the big houses that had been up for sale right on the edge of Willow Point. I'd already heard a couple of them talking about our neighborhood. They called it the slums."

Dad's face got red. "So you pretended you were one of them? You're ashamed of coming from a hard-working family?"

Susan shook her head, but before she could say anything, the phone rang and Mom went to answer it. "George," she called. "Get on the extension, will you? It's Liz's doctor." Dad went upstairs to the other phone, leaving Susan and me at the table.

After a few minutes of silence, Susan said, "I suppose you really hate me now."

"I just can't figure you out, Susan. Why would you want to hang around with those snobs anyway?"

"Well, what was I supposed to do? The girl seemed friendly, and I could tell she was from the most popular group of kids. Besides, I was panicked about not making any friends here."

"You? You don't have any trouble making friends," I said.

"That's how much you know. It isn't easy when you

get the top grades in the class. A lot of people really hate you for that."

"I wouldn't know," I said. "I've never had that problem."

"I know, that's what I mean. You're a regular average kid. You've always had a close friend, like Herbie. Don't you realize I've never had one?"

"You always seemed to have lots of friends in Phillipsburg."

"You're so dense, Ben. What do you think I did with the candy and money I got from you? I had to bribe people to like me."

It made sense, but it would take more than a few candy bars for me to want Susan for a friend.

Susan pulled out a tissue and blew her nose. "Well, you're the big family hero now, Ben. I hope you're satisfied. After all the things you told Mom and Dad, I don't think they'll ever trust me again."

"Sure they will, Susan. They have a real weakness for straight A's. By the end of the first marking period you'll be queen of the household again."

"Thanks a bunch," she said, starting to cry again.

"Look. I'm sorry I said that. It's just hard for me to think of you as anything but a pain in the neck."

Mom came back in from the kitchen smiling. "Liz's doctor said she's doing very well and she could be coming home as early as tomorrow noon."

"That's great, Mom," I said.

"I've missed Liz," Susan said quietly. "It doesn't seem

the same around here without her." Susan looked so sad, I felt sorry for her. She was right. It would be a while before Mom and Dad really trusted her again the way they had before.

Dad came back downstairs. "Well, that was good news. This time tomorrow we'll have everybody back under one roof." He sat down at the table, taking Susan's hand and mine. He took a deep breath and let it out slowly as he looked first at me, then at Susan. "And we're going to start working at being a real family . . . not just five people who live in the same house."

11

Mom and I went back to the hospital that night to see Liz, but she was so sleepy we didn't stay long. The nurse said she needed to get her rest so she could come home the next day.

When we got home, Dad handed me a note. "A friend of yours stopped by and said to give you this. Said her name's Regina."

"Thanks, Dad." I took the note and went over to the chair in the corner to read it. It just said, "Meet me at the beach after school tomorrow — Regina."

"Regina," Mom said. "Why does that name ring a bell? Isn't she the one they mentioned in the newspaper article?"

"I think you're right." Dad went over to shuffle through a pile of newspapers and came up with the one that had my picture on the front. "Regina St. Clair. I'll be darned. Wish I'd known who she was when she was here. We've all been so busy worrying about Liz for the past two days, I'd forgotten about seeing her name in that article. I meant to ask you about her, Ben. She live around here?"

"Sort of."

"What kind of answer is that?"

"She lives on the sandbar. But she's nice, not like Mr. Romano said."

Dad smiled. "Well, Angie has a tendency to exaggerate about some things. You'll have to invite that girl over here so we can thank her for what she did."

Mr. Romano sure hadn't been exaggerating about the witches, though, but I wasn't about to tell Dad. There was a limit to how much I could expect Dad to understand, and I was pretty sure witches were way over that limit.

Witches were almost beyond my limit, too. Regina was my best friend, but it still made me uneasy to picture her stirring up all kinds of magic potions with her grandmother. The next day, I told the soccer coach I had a dentist appointment and got the early bus home. I had to let Regina know I understood about her being a witch. Saving Liz was too big a thing to let slip by without mentioning it. I owed her a lot now, even my life.

In English class we'd been reading about this guy who sold his soul to the devil in exchange for becoming famous. He became a big superstar and everything was great until the devil came back to claim his payment. That story kept going through my mind as I headed out to the beach to find Regina. All this magic stuff had been great for me, and I could do anything I wanted to, just like the guy in the book. But what if I had to pay it all back someday? I tried to imagine Regina telling me it was time to pay up, but it just didn't fit. No, she was helping me because we were friends. It wasn't the same thing at all.

There was no sign of Regina when I got to the beach, so I posted myself at the point to wait. I thought about going out on the sandbar to look for her, but something about the place still gave me the creeps. Dark clouds were rolling in and the wind was whipping up the waves, making them slam into the shore faster than usual. I waited about fifteen minutes more with my hands dug deep in the pockets of my winter jacket, the cold air blowing stronger by the minute. Then the wind slipped an icy finger between my neck and collar and I decided it was time to head for the sandbar, creepy or not.

The wind was at my back, shoving me along the beach with a steady pressure, as if I were being pushed into something. As I was passing behind the shacks, I decided to cut through to the road so I could look for names on mailboxes. The only trouble was that there weren't any mailboxes. I was almost halfway across the sandbar when a strange voice shouted my name.

"Ben! Ben Wagner!"

When I turned around and saw her, I knew immediately who she was. She was old and bent over, her long black dress whipping against her legs in the wind. Her face was twisted, with white hair flying wildly around it and she clutched an old straw broom. It had to be the first Regina, the woman born in the eye of a hurricane and named after a doomed ship. I was standing face to face with a real-life Halloween witch, and I was scared out of my skin. I tried to run, but my feet were frozen to the spot. The old hag was reaching out over the railing of the cottage with a clawlike hand and her lips seemed to be moving, but the wind ripped her words away before they could reach me.

This was it! This was where I was going to pay for all those magic spells. The sky had darkened and the gale began to howl around me. The old witch seemed to be stirring it up. It wasn't fair! I'd never made any deals with Regina. I'd never signed my soul over to anybody.

The wind dropped for a second and I heard the old witch's voice crackling over it. *"Attends! Ne t'en vas pas! Regina te cherche sur la plage."*

It was a strange sort of language, probably an ancient witch's curse, and Regina was mixed up in it somehow. The old hag was obviously trying to turn me into something, and I wasn't going to hang around to find out what! The ground let go of my feet and I shot between two cottages and took off down the beach toward the point.

Black clouds boiled over my head and the wind snatched the breath right out of my throat. I had to get around the other side of the point where the old witch couldn't see me anymore. I swore I'd never have anything to do with Regina again, friend or no friend. I'd been playing with fire all along, and I'd be lucky to get out of this mess without being burned alive.

Just as I dove for safety around the other side of the

point, I ran headlong into Regina, but not the Regina who had been my friend. This girl was wild-eyed and wore a long, black wool cape that fell almost to her ankles. I crouched by the base of the point gasping for breath.

Regina dropped down on her knees beside me. "Ben, I was looking for you. What's wrong?"

I put both hands up in front of me. "I know everything now, Regina, so stop pretending you don't know what's going on."

"What are you talking about?"

"I saw her, Regina."

"Who?"

"Your grandmother. I know what you're both trying to do, but I didn't make any deals with you or sign anything. So it's not legal."

"What deals? Ben, you're not making any sense. Calm down."

"Calm down!" I shouted. "That old hag tried to put a curse on me."

"Who are you calling an old hag?"

"Your grandmother. I know what she is, and you too. And I'm grateful for all the help you gave me, especially for saving Liz, but just because you're a witch, that doesn't give you the right —"

"A witch!" Regina stood up suddenly, her eyes practically shooting sparks. As I looked up at her from the ground, she seemed very tall and powerful. Her black cape caught in a sudden gust and billowed out behind her, its corners cracking like whips. The wind had blown her

123

hair into an eerie halo against the dark greenish sky. She looked like a younger version of her grandmother, but every bit as dangerous. She raised her hand and pointed a shaking finger at me. I ducked my head, hoping she couldn't do anything to me if I didn't look into her eyes.

"Ben Wagner!" she wailed over the shrieking wind. I just crouched there with my eyes squeezed shut, waiting for something to happen. There was nothing but the sound of the wind and my heartbeat, going a mile a minute. Still, nothing happened. Maybe Regina wasn't a full-fledged witch yet. Maybe she was an apprentice to her grandmother and couldn't really zap anybody. The wind dropped again, and I could hear crying. I opened my eyes and saw Regina leaning against the rock wall of the point with tears running down her cheeks. Was this another trick?

Regina saw me look up. She wiped her eyes quickly with the back of her hand and jutted out her chin. "Ben Wagner, you're the most hateful person I've ever met! I don't know why I ever liked you at all. I'm sure you've hurt my grandmother's feelings."

That was too much. "Hurt her feelings? Are you crazy? I know who your grandmother is. She's the witch of the sandbar. And she's teaching you to be a witch too, right?"

"Don't be ridiculous."

"Come on, Regina, I know all about it. Mr. Romano told me. He warned me not to have anything to do with you people, but I was too stupid to listen."

Regina's eyes narrowed and she looked at me for a few

seconds. "You're serious, aren't you? You really believe all that superstitious nonsense about witches."

"I didn't, but I do now. It's so obvious."

"What's obvious?"

"Well, you, for one thing. Look at the way you're dressed. How many twelve-year-old girls go around wearing long black capes?"

"None, I hope. I told you I like to be different. But being different doesn't make me a witch. This isn't Salem, you know."

"Well, maybe not, but there were lots of other strange things. You turned yourself into a dog once, and a cat another time. I suppose you have a logical explanation for that?"

"I never did any such thing," Regina said, pulling the cape tight around herself.

Why was she lying about it? Maybe it was a crime for a witch to reveal herself to a normal person. I kept at her. "Oh, yes you did, right on this spot, as a matter of fact. The first couple of times I saw you down here, you ran away from me, then changed into an animal. You're not going to deny that, are you? Because I saw it happen with my own eyes."

"But I never. . . ." A flicker of understanding crossed Regina's face. "Wait a minute. I don't know anything about the animals, but I can show you how I disappeared. Follow me."

She led me around to the sandbar side of the point and ducked down behind a scrubby bush that clung to its base. Now that was stupid. I knew she hadn't been hiding behind any scrawny little bush the other times. She had . . . geez! She wasn't behind the bush now, either. She'd disappeared again. This sure was a strange way for her to prove she wasn't a witch.

"Ben, over here." Regina's head and shoulders were sticking out of a small, arched opening at the base of the point. I couldn't believe I'd never noticed it before. "Come on in, Ben. It's nice and cozy in here."

"Is this a trick?"

"Will you stop with that nonsense? Just crawl through the opening."

I ducked down and crawled through, but stayed close to the opening when I got inside. It was a small cave, barely high enough to stand up in, with walls carved out of rock. There was a big, fat candle burning on a ledge. The melting wax sizzled as it dripped into the cracks of the damp rock. As the flickering candle cast weird moving shadows on the walls, I could see tiny twin flames burning in Regina's eyes. This definitely was not my idea of cozy.

Regina sat cross-legged in the center of the cave floor, the black cape spreading out around her. "This is my secret place. Only the sandbar people know about it. Each time you chased me, I ducked in here. The animals you saw had nothing to do with me. That must have been coincidence."

"Oh, yeah? Well I don't think this cave was even here before, because I would've seen it. I think you just zapped it up right now." I started to edge closer to the entrance.

126

I had the strangest sensation that Regina was two people, my old friend and this witch-person. She kept seeming to slip back and forth between the two.

Regina's eyes flashed in the candlelight. "How am I going to get it through your thick head? I'm not a witch. I don't know how to zap anything." Then she leaned toward me and her voice softened. "Come on, Ben. Let's calm down and talk this over, so we can get things straightened out."

"Okay," I said, not letting down my guard. "Start explaining."

"All right. For one thing, this cave has been here for ages. Whoever dug it out carved the opening so it looked like a shadow in the rock. Now that you've seen it, you'll be amazed that you never noticed it before."

"All right, never mind the cave. If you're not a witch, how do you make your eyes change color all the time?"

Regina laughed. "You've got to be kidding. I don't do anything to change my eyes. They just look different in different light, I guess. Sometimes they seem to change, depending on what color I'm wearing. A lot of people have eyes like that. It's probably because they're a very light color."

"Well, what about your grandmother and you mixing up all those magic potions out of weeds and plants?"

"I never said they were magic potions."

"You called them brews or confusions or something. That sounds pretty witchy to me."

Regina laughed. "Infusions, Ben, and they're not witchy. You make an infusion by steeping dried leaves

127

in hot water. Tea is an infusion. Does that sound sinister to you?"

"I guess not, but I still think it's weird to mess with that stuff."

"Look, my grandmother learned herbal medicine as a girl. It's been passed down in our family for generations and has nothing to do with witches."

"All right. I guess I could go along with that, but there's no way you can explain away the magic spells."

"What magic spells?"

"You know darn well what I'm talking about. It was your eyes. You'd look at me and then I'd get that strange feeling. Like the time I was trying to cross that stream on the log, and I almost fell off. You put a spell on me and saved me."

"But I just. . ."

"Let me finish. Then there was the spell that got me on the soccer team, and the one so I could talk to my teachers, and the biggest one of all was the spell that helped me rescue Liz. Now I couldn't have done any one of those things without some sort of magic, so don't deny you made it happen."

"How do you think I did it?"

"I told you. You'd stare at me. Then you'd say, 'I know you can do it.' "

"And then you did it."

"That's right."

"That's exactly right, Ben. You did it. It wasn't magic spells or witches. It was you."

"That's impossible. It even said in the paper that I

shouldn't have been able to swim in those waves and rescue Liz. I'm not even that great a swimmer. I was practically drowning until you yelled at me. That's why I never felt good about all that hero stuff, because without the magic, Liz and I would have drowned."

"Look, Ben. Did I put any sort of spell on you before you dove off that pier?"

"No. That's why I was having such a hard time."

"You dove off the pier, swam all the way over to where Liz was, then swam with her all the way past the jetty, in four-foot waves, without any spell at all, right?"

"Yeah, I guess so."

"Can you explain that?"

"Not really, but . . ."

"I can explain it, Ben. It took courage to dive off that pier, and you did it because your little sister was drowning. You wanted to save her, even if it meant risking your own life."

"How could I do all that on my own, without any magic?"

"You make me crazy, Ben. You believe that I can give you power — magic power. It would be a lot easier for you if I just said I was a witch, wouldn't it? Then you wouldn't have to look at the truth."

"What *is* the truth?"

"The truth is, you're responsible for what happens to you. Both the good and the bad. I didn't give you any magic power. You've always been able to do those things. You just didn't think you could. All I did was try to give you some encouragement. You did all the rest. Just stop believing in witches and start believing in yourself. That's where the magic is."

We sat for a long time in the flickering yellow light. The only sounds were the hiss of hot wax splattering on the stone ledge and the distant howl of the wind. I let my mind sift and sort through all of Regina's explanations. Finally, she spoke. "Do you believe me, Ben?"

"Yeah, I guess so."

She got up and reached out her hand. "Come on. I want you to meet my grandmother."

"Wait a minute. Okay, so you're not a witch, but your grandmother was yelling a curse at me."

"What did she say?"

"How should I know? It was in some ancient witch language."

Regina smiled and shook her head. "French, Ben. When Grandmother tries to say something in a hurry, it comes out in French. She was probably trying to tell you that I went out to meet you. Storms upset her."

"She was upset, all right. And she sure looked like a witch."

"She's a very gentle old woman, Ben. Besides, the way your imagination was running wild, your own mother would have looked like a witch to you."

"Yeah, maybe you're right," I said, following her out of the cave.

The sunshine was moving toward us down the beach. The wind had died down, but the air still had a bite to it.

"Regina, about this witch thing. Can we keep that just between the two of us?"

She was kicking at stones, looking for good skippers as we walked along the beach. "What's the matter, Ben? Embarrassed?"

"Look, anybody could have made the same mistake. There was a lot of evidence pointing to the fact that you were a witch."

"Oh, Ben. You sound like a lawyer. Don't worry. I'm not going to say anything to anybody."

"Promise?"

"I promise," Regina said, crossing her heart, with a funny little smile on her face. She flipped a stone into the water and it did the usual spectacular skip.

I threw one, about the three millionth stone I'd winged into Lake Ontario, and the lake lapped it up after the second skip. "Can't you explain to me how you make it jump a wave?" I asked. "It's driving me nuts."

"I think it's in the timing, Ben, but if I slow it down to figure it out, I can't do it myself. You must be trying too hard. Just relax and don't think about it so much. I know you can do it."

I took a deep breath and shook the tension out of my arms. Then I wound up and, without thinking about it, I let one fly. Zing! One-two-three-four, up and over, one-two-three-four!

"I did it!" I shouted, scaring the heck out of a seagull that was circling low overhead. "I really did it! I finally, actually did it!"

Regina watched my stone until it sank out of sight. Then she turned back to me very slowly, with that strange little smile.

"No, you didn't," she said. "I zapped you!"